Words and Dreams

by

Laura Strickland

A Sequel to Forged by Love

Words and Dreams

Cover Art by *Diana Carlile*

The Wild Rose Press, Inc.
PO Box 708
Adams Basin, NY 14410-0708
Visit us at www.thewildrosepress.com

Publishing History
First American Rose Edition, 2017
Print ISBN 978-1-5092-1326-9
Digital ISBN 978-1-5092-1327-6

A Sequel to Forged by Love
Published in the United States of America

Dorothea reached for the hat, but like the rascal he undoubtedly was, he kept it from her grasp, pretending to examine it closely. He brushed off a bit of grit from the brim and fingered the now-tattered veil.

"A mite worse for its adventure, but no doubt you can mend it, women having a certain magical talent for such things."

Again Dorothea reached for her hat; again he kept it from her only to take a step closer and set it on her head.

"There you go, beautiful lady. You will be sure and hold on to it more closely next time."

Dorothea, assaulted by the full force of his masculinity, said nothing, though she reached up one hand and clamped the hat to her head. She looked into his face, and all the breath fled her lungs.

He wore no cap and had a headful of copper curls well-tossed by the wind. His face screamed Ireland, with a broad forehead and slightly squared jaw, all sprinkled with freckles visible even beneath his worker's tan. His eyes—but no. Dorothea met them once before her gaze skittered away much as the hat had, only to return again on a rush of fascination.

Tawny gold as those of a tomcat, his eyes held a world of emotions: amusement first of all, that flaming confidence, an uncanny wisdom, and a hint of daring. Dorothea responded to the last first—seldom did she fail to accept a dare.

Praise for Laura Strickland

"I was so caught up and excited to find out the outcome, but still a part of me didn't want the story to end. The author has a talent for writing and telling a story that is sure to capture readers."

~Ginger, Long and Short Reviews

~*~

"I didn't know if Ms. Strickland would give them a HEA or an HFN with this being a short story, but I didn't want to stop reading, and could happily have read this as a longer story if she ever chose to rewrite and expand it."

~Honeysuckle at Long and Short Reviews

Chapter One

Boston, Massachusetts, May 1871

Dorothea Sinclair gazed out at the far-reaching sweep of the broad Atlantic, hoping the inshore wind might chase the heat from her flushed cheeks. A roiling mass of embarrassment, anger, and indignation filled her heart to overflowing, each emotion warring for dominance. Even worse, the devil known as self-doubt gnawed at her with small, insistent teeth.

Curse it all, but she couldn't allow herself to fail in the course she'd set. She had worked, hoped, and planned far too long for this opportunity, and she'd be darned if she'd creep back home with her tail between her legs.

Home. The very word sapped some of her rage and allowed longing to take its place. The last thing she'd expected after finally springing herself from the small town in Maine where she'd been born and raised was homesickness. But as an honest woman she had to admit she missed it all: the noise of the little house on the shore, filled to overflowing with her younger brothers and her parents' dog, Chieftain. Her mother's cooking; her steady patience in the face of all things, and the feeling of safety that accompanied her father when he came home from work in the forge at the end of the day.

She ached for it all, sharp and real as a barb to her heart.

Nothing about Boston felt safe: not the rooming house where she lived or the crowded streets. Not even the newspaper office where she worked.

Especially after today.

How could she ever go back there again? Yet she'd worked so hard for this chance—and talked it up at length back home. She couldn't give up, either.

The wind blew harder and rocked her on the balls of her feet. To think she'd expected to become a successful newspaper woman within three months, with a byline and a credible reputation. Instead she found herself a dogsbody with even less clout than the boys who carried the papers, subjected to any humiliation.

Including advances from the chief editor's son.

Dorothea chewed her lower lip and asked herself what she meant to do about it. A resourceful woman, she'd met many a challenge in the past with a combination of forthrightness and determination. Was she about to let a toad-faced, weedy, evil-minded snob like Jeremy Winton derail her future?

She had no doubt Jeremy Winton was a snob of the first water—and worse. Supposed to be assisting his father, Montgomery Winton, in running the *Guardian*, Dorothea hadn't seen him do a lick of actual work in all the weeks she'd been there. When he did show up— rarely enough—he stood around braying, boasting about the social events he'd attended and bragging about the regatta team he captained, lately all while keeping an eye cocked in Dorothea's direction. Though he'd made her uncomfortable from the start, today had been the first time he'd sneaked past her defenses and caught her alone. And what he'd said then...

Dorothea's face burned anew, defying the cool wind off the ocean. She should have slapped him right then and there, she really should. But one couldn't slap Montgomery Winton's son and expect to keep one's job. That would have been it, and she'd be crawling off home before she knew it.

She blinked furiously against the sting of the wind—she wouldn't allow it as anything more—and tried desperately to garner some peace from the broad Atlantic. The sea was the sea—here or at home. And that meant she really wasn't so far from her parents, her brothers, and her best friend, Jo Grier.

But by heaven, something had to happen that would turn things around for her.

Upon that thought, the wind gusted harder and lifted the hat she wore straight off her head. Before Dorothea could react, the bonnet turned three somersaults and scuttled away along the waterfront where she stood, heading westward.

She spoke a word no gently raised young woman should know and set off in pursuit. She loved that hat; before coming to Boston, she'd saved her money for weeks to afford it and had helped Jo Grier—a talented seamstress—trim it up with blue ribbons and clusters of forget-me-nots that matched the color of Dorothea's eyes. It had a sweet little half-veil in the front and, Dorothea felt, made her look older than her twenty years. When it came to sophistication, she needed all the help she could get.

She might have had one of the worst days of her career, but curse it all, she wouldn't lose that hat!

The waterfront here in south Boston, as she rather

belatedly realized, lay nearly deserted, and the sun rapidly sank to the west behind the crowded buildings. She'd stood here far too long trying to gather up her courage, and now most of the workers and other folk had gone home to supper.

At Mrs. Bennett's boarding house, the food would already be laid on the long, scarred table. And not enough of it. Agnes Bennett ran her house with a miserly attention to cost. A boarder had to be on time and quick with a serving spoon to get her fill.

Dorothea nearly groaned as her hat, the little veil fluttering, came to a halt on a round cobblestone and then, just as she bent to snag it, took off again, tumbling still faster toward the barrier that fronted the road.

She would likely lose her hat *and* miss her supper.

Plus she'd have to walk all the way back to Mrs. Bennett's in the half-darkness, never a safe bet for a woman alone.

The hat caught on the barrier and teased her by stopping just long enough for her to stoop and brush it with her fingers. This time when she bent down, her hair loosened and blew around her face in a black curtain that obscured her vision.

The blue hat sailed up and over the barrier, and Dorothea, determined now beyond all reason, scrambled after it in a tangle of bombazine skirt.

Somehow, in her mind, the hat had come to represent everything—her future here in Boston, her success, her ability to fulfill her dreams.

The hat blew into the road, where a carriage barely missed it. The horse reared and faltered; the driver shook his fist at Dorothea. The hat tumbled across and reached the other side.

There…Dorothea didn't know from whence the man appeared, but he did so just in time to swoop and snatch up her hat before it moved onward.

Half grateful and wholly exasperated, she studied him, and her eyes and her heart fell. Oh, no, a ruffian.

She'd been well-advised since arriving in Boston to avoid men just like this. Mrs. Bennett had warned her, as had Molly, the female typesetter at the *Guardian* and, initially, Montgomery Winton himself. Riffraff, folks tended to call such men, and endemic in Boston, where a wide gulf existed between the established community and the Irish incomers.

And, if she was Dorothea Sinclair, this man must be Irish. His heritage lay upon him like a brand, visible even in the fading light. From his clothing, he must be a working man—or worse.

He sported a long leather coat, well-scuffed and worn open to show a pair of rough trousers and a workman's shirt, unbuttoned at the throat.

Nothing wrong in that. Dorothea's own father was a workman, if a skilled one—the blacksmith back home. This man had no blacksmith's build. Instead he looked light on his feet, square-shouldered, and graceful as quicksilver. Brash confidence rolled off him in waves.

As she stood staring across the road in consternation, he held up her hat and grinned before casting a look both ways and jogging over to her side.

He brought a presence with him that backed Dorothea up a step or two. She might credit it to the set of those fine shoulders or the grin that still occupied his face or the swagger he displayed that made the most of his height, which, surely, didn't top six feet.

He reached her, spent an instant examining her closely, and presented her hat with a sweeping bow worthy of a practiced thespian.

"Lovely miss, I'm thinking this belongs to you."

"Yes. Yes, it does, thank you."

Dorothea reached for the hat, but like the rascal he undoubtedly was, he kept it from her grasp, pretending to examine it closely. He brushed off a bit of grit from the brim and fingered the now-tattered veil.

"A mite worse for its adventure, but no doubt you can mend it, women having a certain magical talent for such things."

Again Dorothea reached for her hat; again he kept it from her only to take a step closer and set it on her head.

"There you go, beautiful lady. You will be sure and hold on to it more closely next time."

Dorothea, assaulted by the full force of his masculinity, said nothing, though she reached up one hand and clamped the hat to her head. She looked into his face, and all the breath fled her lungs.

He wore no cap and had a headful of copper curls well-tossed by the wind. His face screamed Ireland, with a broad forehead and slightly squared jaw, all sprinkled with freckles visible even beneath his worker's tan. His eyes—but no. Dorothea met them once before her gaze skittered away much as the hat had, only to return again on a rush of fascination.

Tawny gold as those of a tomcat, his eyes held a world of emotions: amusement first of all, that flaming confidence, an uncanny wisdom, and a hint of daring. Dorothea responded to the last first—seldom did she fail to accept a dare.

He examined her in turn, just as curiously. The tawny eyes, fringed by copper lashes and set beneath brows as mobile as runaway commas, moved to her hair, then to her mouth, where they lingered before returning to her eyes.

"Lovely, indeed," he said in a voice like warm honey. "But surely you know you shouldn't be here on your own, not with night coming on."

"Night wasn't coming on when I arrived."

"Aye, well, time has marched along." His accent, not overtly Irish after all, owed more to phrasing than inflection. But its timbre sounded seductive as a promise. "It's not safe for you to be alone here. Where were you bound?"

A good question. She should make for the rooming house like a frightened mouse; she wanted, with surprising intensity, to go home to Maine.

Her only reply, though, came in the form of a loud rumble from her stomach.

His face filled with laughter and warmth. "Well, now, and you should be bound home for your dinner."

The laughter breeched Dorothea's defenses as nothing else could. She relaxed marginally.

"I fear I am too late. The board will already be laid at the house where I'm staying, and all the food—of meager proportion as it is—disappearing even now down half a score of gullets."

"You are not from Boston. You cannot have been here long—such a flower could not bloom here and I not knowing."

"I'm from Maine, actually," Dorothea admitted, the color flooding her cheeks again.

"Maine, eh?" Did some of the light in his

extraordinary eyes dim? "And what might you be doing in this great, wicked city?"

"Working. There aren't a lot of good opportunities back home."

He took a half step back and eyed her up and down. "Let me guess—you're working at the university, one of the girls who take the tea cart round."

"I am not! And, if I may say so, that's quite insulting." Though she'd been asked to run and fetch tea more than once, at the newspaper office. "Is that what I look like to you?"

"You look like the bonniest thing I've ever seen, if you want the truth. And me, I never lie to a beautiful woman."

Dorothea rolled her eyes, and he grinned again.

"I gather, Miss Lovely, you are not beguiled by my silver tongue."

Oh, she was beguiled, all right. But she said tartly, "On the contrary, sir, you remind me of my younger brothers, who will say anything to win their way. Well," she amended swiftly, "Andrew doesn't say much yet, him still being an infant." Andrew had been a surprise to her parents last Christmas, albeit a welcome one. "But Alastair and Archie could give you a run for your money."

"Ah, then. I'm thinking your name will also start with an A. Angela, perhaps, as befits such a heavenly vision."

Oh, he was quick! "I assure you, I am no angel. And neither does my name start with an A."

He cocked his head as if awaiting further enlightenment. When she buttoned her lip and failed to elucidate, he said, "To be sure, the true sin is that your parents produced only one daughter, and you pretty enough to rival the moon."

"Blarney," Dorothea pronounced, but couldn't defeat the smile that tugged at her lips.

He laid his hand on his heart and bowed again. "Perhaps you will do me the honor of letting me see you home."

"Well, I don't know."

"Or better yet, since you fear the vultures at your rooming house will have eaten all the grub, you'll let me buy you some supper."

"Oh, I don't think that's a good idea."

He ignored her protest as if it didn't exist. "I know a fine little place—not in the best neighborhood, perhaps, but the grub makes up for it." He drew himself up and offered his arm. "Come now, Miss Angel; you can't expect me to abandon you here on your own, and me a gentleman."

Chapter Two

Gentleman? Dorothea narrowed her eyes. Whatever the man standing in front of her might be— dangerously attractive from his wild head of hair to his scuffed boots—he could not be considered a gentleman.

She cleared her throat. "I couldn't possibly trouble you, sir. Surely you have business here on the waterfront. You must be in the area for some reason."

"I came to meet a man, but he'll wait on me. They always do."

Such arrogance! But he wore it well.

"I assure you, I can see myself home. It's not the first time I've been out after dark."

"Then if you will forgive me saying, you must be as foolish as you are beautiful." He wagged his crooked arm suggestively. "I would not let my sister out in this neighborhood unaccompanied."

"You have a sister?"

"Well, no." The smile flashed again.

Oh, blast, Dorothea thought. What was she to do? Would it be so terrible to let him see her home? Of course, the supper invitation went beyond consideration.

Didn't it?

He leaned closer, his voice a mere whisper aimed at her ear. "But if I did have a sister, I'd hope she'd be like you. No, but wait—that would be purely sinful."

Dorothea, although trying to take offense at such suggestiveness, laughed instead.

"Very well, I'll accept your escort. Just let me try and do something with my hair first."

She handed him back the hat, clawed the streaming hair from her eyes, and gathered it all between her hands. Still fighting the force of the wind, she gave the heavy tresses a twist and secured them with the one or two hairpins she could locate. Last of all, she accepted the hat and crammed it on.

"There now," he crooned, "a real lady."

When he extended his elbow yet again, she accepted it, and they started away, their steps matching perfectly.

"I should not go anywhere with you, sir," Dorothea said, "lest you tell me your name."

"I can tell you *a* name." He slanted a look at her. "Folks call me O'Hare."

"O'Hare!" Dorothea stopped walking abruptly and stared. "*The* O'Hare?"

She'd heard of him—a personage of some fame in south Boston, he'd been denounced as a scoundrel, a rebel, a leader of the near-militant Irish labor force that plagued the city. The *Guardian* had run more than one story decrying his activities and those of his cohorts, as well as any number of letters sent in by angry Boston residents, denouncing him. There'd been some ugly incidents: confrontations with young Anglo toffs, protests staged outside businesses, some of which had turned violent, and even a series of fires.

But now he turned to her and smiled as charmingly as if she'd just paid him a grand compliment.

"He, and no other. I see you've heard of me,

11

Angel. I'm flattered."

"Your fame does rather precede you." Dorothea's thoughts flew with the speed of which they were sometimes capable. Was she safe in this man's company? Could she turn his presence somehow to her advantage? Might this encounter be an opportunity?

For all the denouncements and rather dubious fame, no one had successfully interviewed this man. Indeed, Dorothea had heard Mr. Winton bemoaning that very fact to one of his top reporters just yesterday.

Dorothea needed an exclusive, an interview that would thrust her to the forefront of her chosen profession, make her employer take her seriously.

And she just might have the means right here on her arm.

O'Hare may not like the idea, but when necessity dictated, she could be just as persuasive as he.

She gave him her best smile. "Mr. O'Hare, perhaps I will accept your supper invitation after all."

****

O'Hare blinked as the raven-haired beauty turned the full power of her smile on him. Well, and she had changed her mind with astonishing speed at learning his identity. He wondered if he should be alarmed but dismissed the possibility. No woman so innocently lovely could have unscrupulous intentions.

Sure, even without the smile she was enough to steal his breath: skin pure as pearl, with all that black hair in sharp contrast, and a pair of blue-gray eyes so dreamy and fey he scarcely dared look into them.

He'd wooed many a beauty, from one end of Boston to the other, most of them lightskirts, a few actual ladies, and had learned a lot about women along

12

the way—what they liked, what they didn't, and how to talk them into damn near anything. A smile and a bit of the Irish generally did the trick. Women just liked him, despite his reputation. He didn't ask why.

But he'd never seen a lass to match the one beside him, who'd reclaimed his arm and resumed walking as if they strolled through a summer's day instead of an ink-black, windy waterfront night.

"Well, now," he said softly, "and isn't that wonderful news?"

He could feel heat radiating from the place where her arm looped through his and from her side as well, pressed close. He didn't doubt her for a lady—one hundred percent. But she might as well be a seductress for the effect she was having on him.

Caution, lad, he told himself. He could afford to be nobody's fool.

"And might I ask why you've decided to accept?"

She cast another of those looks at him, brimming with intelligence. Him not being a particularly tall man, she came to the top of his ear.

Just the right height for kissing.

"I'm hungry," she confessed with disarming frankness. "Where's this restaurant?"

"Not far. If I'm to take you to supper, might I have the honor of knowing your name?"

"I don't see why not. I'm Dorothea Sinclair, and I'm a reporter for the *Guardian*."

O'Hare stiffened with dismay. Ah, and he knew there had to be a catch. Hooked like a fish and in over his head was he?

"That rag sheet!" he exclaimed in disgust. "They never print anything that isn't either sensational or serving the elite of this city. And since when have they begun hiring female reporters?"

"What's wrong with that, Mr. O'Hare? I would think you, of all people, would embrace equal opportunities for everyone. Isn't that what your campaign in this city is all about?"

"It is," he conceded. "Equal pay and treatment despite class, place of birth—or gender. But I can tell you, Miss Sinclair, you won't find any of that while working at the *Guardian*."

"A person has to take her opportunities where she finds them."

Aye, so, and had she decided he offered an opportunity? He hoped not. He liked her and wouldn't want to slap her down.

He clucked his tongue. "Is that why you were standing there on the dockside looking as if you wanted to jump into the ocean?" And why he saw evidence of dried tears on her cheeks, though he certainly wouldn't mention those.

She faltered, and her toe caught on a stone underfoot. O'Hare's arm kept her from stumbling.

"Yes, well," she said, "you may have caught me at a weak moment. The struggle for equality isn't an easy one, as I'm sure you agree."

An unexpected wave of protectiveness surged up through him. He didn't make a habit of coddling women—his ma had taught him better than that. Women were for charming and sometimes for using— ultimately they cared only for themselves.

She went on determinedly, "I did not have a particularly good day. I'm afraid homesickness overtook me for a moment or two."

He snorted. "Being homesick's a fool's game. Take my advice and deal with the moment. Don't look too far ahead, and never, never look back."

And who was he to be giving advice?

She shot him yet another of those looks that seemed to see right through him. Damn it, he wouldn't have said he found intelligence arousing—till now.

He decided he might just as well relax and enjoy himself—take his own counsel and live in the moment. What harm could she do him, after all, a wee slip of a thing?

"How much farther, Mr. O'Hare?"

"We're almost there. And as I say, it's not 'Mr.' O'Hare—just O'Hare, sure."

"Not your real name but a moniker, correct?"

"What's that, when it's at home?"

"Just a title you've given yourself."

"You make me sound like a pretender."

"I don't think that at all. Your story is both fascinating and edifying. Well worthy of a grandiose title, certainly."

He quirked an eyebrow. "Are you saying you find me inspiring?"

"Oh, very much so." She launched into a lengthy diatribe about the books she'd read—extreme enough in number to fill a library, from the sound of it—and the heroes in them. Well, if she'd come looking for a hero, she searched in the wrong place.

And by heaven, how she could talk! He didn't follow half of it but had to admit he liked the sound of her voice and the way she leaned into him at specific moments. Did she even know her high, rounded breast touched his arm?

He interrupted her flow of words by pausing in front of the Golden Cockrell, or rather she interrupted herself to exclaim, "What's this place?"

"Our supper house."

"But"—she looked aghast—"it's a tavern."

"More or less. There's a room in back where the proprietress, Miss Eunice, serves food. Families go there all the time." Of course they were the kind of families with whom this wee flower likely never associated. He need not tell her that.

"I can't go into such a place!" She sounded appalled.

He shrugged. "You'll have to venture into far worse places, chasing stories."

"You're right." She cast him another searing look. "And I imagine I'll be safe in your company."

O'Hare's knees promptly went weak. What magic did she have that affected him so? He usually took women and their ploys with a healthy grain of salt.

He barely recognized himself, with Miss Dorothea Sinclair on his arm.

With tongue-in-cheek gallantry, he returned, "Sure, and would I not lay down my life for your honor? Come away in."

A wall of light and noise hit them as they stepped through the door of the Cockrell. Barely dark and the place already hopped with activity. Men—all clad just as roughly as O'Hare—crowded the long, polished bar to the right.

Women, many of them lightskirts, chatted up fellows at the tables to the left. O'Hare wondered if Miss Sinclair could tell the ladies' profession. Him, he felt comfortable around such women. His own mother had earned her living thus, back when he was very young.

Heads turned all over the room when he came in, and cries of greeting sang out. "O'Hare!" And some just, "Hare!" along with one or two, "Darling lad!" from women he'd bedded in the past.

Curious eyes focused on the woman beside him. Even with the tattered hat back on her head and her black hair only more or less bundled beneath it, she screamed *class*. A rarity, here.

And why bring her to such a place? Did he want to shock her? Maybe. Also, Eunice served up good food he could afford.

He caught Eunice's eye and jerked his chin at the back room. She nodded in return.

Hopefully it would be quiet in there. But first they had to cross the big room, where conversation had died to a murmur and everybody stared.

Get a good look at her, boys—this one's under my protection.

Miss Sinclair clutched his arm so hard he bet she left bruises, but she showed no other sign of agitation. Head high, she sailed like a neat little sloop past the moored boats tethered in the harbor. Aye—with him, a right scow, at her side.

He heard her breathe a sigh when they reached the relative seclusion of the back room. Not large, the room held but six tables. Two men sat at one, in close conversation.

O'Hare eyed them before choosing a table as far away as possible, and pulled out Miss Sinclair's chair like a gentleman.

"Well," she said once seated, "this isn't so bad."

"Wait till you taste the fare. And we can talk here with a bit of privacy. You can present your proposal to me."

She stared at him. "How did you know—?"

"Ah, come, Miss Sinclair. I am no fool. You wish to make your way up at the *Guardian*. And reporters all over the city have been angling for an interview with me."

She looked relieved. "Then you are not opposed to the idea? You'll give me an exclusive?"

"I didn't say that."

Eunice O'Riley entered the room, leading with her magnificent chest. "Well, well, if it isn't the most charming man in the city of Boston come to grace my lowly establishment. To what do I owe the honor?"

"I've been talking up your wondrous food, treasure. We're very hungry. What would you recommend tonight?"

"Well." Eunice eyed Miss Sinclair. "I'm fresh out of oysters, if you were hoping."

"Me? Hope? You know better than that."

"Aye, well, I've a fine bit of salt beef and potatoes, with pumpkin chutney. The best, as you say, in south Boston."

"In all Boston," O'Hare corrected.

"Ale first?"

"I'll have a pint. My lady?" he raised an eyebrow at Miss Sinclair.

"Oh, I'm afraid not. I don't drink."

Conversation at the other table ceased. Eunice stared at Miss Sinclair as if she'd just sprouted antlers.

"Do tell?"

"Bring her a wee cordial," O'Hare told Eunice.

"Just to take the chill from her bones."

Eunice crooked an eyebrow but made no objection and sailed off. Conversation at the other table resumed.

"Cordial?" Miss Sinclair began. "I hardly think—"

"A word of advice, darlin'. If you're chasing down a story on the other fellow's turf, you don't make yourself stand out in any way, understand? Refusing a drink in this place makes you stand out like a beacon on a dark hilltop."

"Yes, I quite understand. Thank you."

"Oh, I'm full of wisdom, me." He gave her his best smile. "Now why don't you convince me I should grant you an interview?"

Chapter Three

Dorothea drew a deep breath and eyed the man who sat opposite her. He lounged back in his chair, one leg propped on the opposite knee and one hand dangling across his lap, to all appearances perfectly at ease. How she could tell it for pantomime, she couldn't say except she felt his tension, like a coiled spring. He might play at nonchalance, and amusement might fill those uncanny golden eyes, but something more lurked beneath.

She figured she had half an hour—or however long it took them to consume their meal—to convince him. No use wasting time or words.

"Very well." She placed her fingers on the table. "Let me tell you a story."

One of his mobile eyebrows twitched. "A story, is it?"

"Yes. When I was young, I wanted most desperately to be an author. Well, I still do. Like Louisa May Alcott. Have you heard—?"

"Oh, aye."

"Well, I worked hard in school and wrote a lot of stories, which my teacher helped me enter in competitions. I won a few." More than a few, but he didn't need to know that. "And I completed a novel, but when I sent it to publishers—some right here in Boston—it went nowhere." She frowned. "I always had

20

it returned with rejection letters, some polite and some not very. One offered genuine advice, saying I had talent but needed more life experience. He suggested a career in journalism to build a foundation."

O'Hare traced a pattern on the table with one graceful brown finger. "What's your novel about?"

Dorothea lit with genuine pleasure. "My best friend back in Maine—it's her love story. She's a very special person, you see."

O'Hare wrinkled his nose. "Why don't you write something with a bit more meat to it, adventure and danger…about an orphan, maybe, who makes good."

"That's been done. Anyway"—Dorothea touched her bosom—"I have to write what's in my heart."

His tawny gaze followed her fingers, warm as a touch. "I see."

"Anyway, I took the publisher's advice and wrote to newspapers all around, stating my credentials and asking them to consider me for a place. Imagine my astonishment when the *Guardian* replied favorably."

"Imagine."

Eunice returned to the room, carrying a frothing mug and a small glass, both of which she set on the table.

O'Hare lifted his drink and drained half of it in a single go, which made Dorothea blink at him. She hoped he didn't mean to get drunk. How would she find her way home from here?

"Food will be right out," Eunice told O'Hare. She walked off, and he nodded at Dorothea's glass. "Try it."

The liquid in the glass shone red like a melted ruby, and the glass looked relatively clean. Dorothea lifted it to her lips, watched closely by O'Hare.

21

"Oh, my. Cherry."

He smiled, and warmth flooded her again, matched by what spilled down her throat. Potent stuff, but with such a small glass, what harm could it do?

"Well, now, where was I?"

"Contacted by the *Guardian*," O'Hare drawled. "Did you come for an interview?"

"They didn't ask for one. Or rather, I suppose I was interviewed via correspondence. They eventually offered me the place. You cannot imagine how excited I was—how excited my family was for me."

"All the lads whose names start with A."

"And my parents. I arranged to room at Mrs. Bennett's—also by letter—and came to Boston. That was three months ago."

"Ever been to Boston before?"

"Oh, yes." Once, but she needn't tell him that. She with her mother, Jo, and her mother's friend Mrs. Becker had traveled down to purchase some yard goods that her mother and Jo, both seamstresses, needed for a special project. They'd stayed at a nice hotel and had tea. Miles from this place where she now sat—miles from Mrs. Bennett's boarding house, for all that.

"Let me guess; when you got here, the job at the *Guardian* proved a disappointment."

"Yes. I got no actual writing assignments and was set to editing other reporters' copy, reading miles of newsprint till my eyes crossed. That or fetching and carrying for the staff and Mr. Winton's vile son. Mr. Winton is—"

"The head man, aye. Go on."

"To say I was disappointed is an understatement. I'd talked it all up so much back home, you see. Said I had a place on a fine Boston paper and would soon be a published novelist."

She took another sip of cordial, bigger this time. Her eyes watered, but oh, she did like that warm feeling. However, the drink seemed to sit strangely on her empty stomach and definitely loosened her tongue.

She leaned across the table impulsively. "How can I return home and admit I've failed?"

"And have you failed?"

She licked a bit of sticky sweetness off her lip, aware of how his gaze followed the movement of her tongue. "This cordial is very good, isn't it?"

"The best in Boston. But tell me, darlin', do you want to go home?"

He really shouldn't call her "darlin'," but she couldn't worry about that now. "No. Yes. Well, that's pretty much what I was contemplating when my hat blew off."

"I thought as much."

"You see, I'm quite determined to triumph—I've always been very determined."

"I can see that."

"But I had something of a setback at the paper today. Mr. Winton has a son."

"So you mentioned. Anyway, I've heard of him. Bit of a rake and ne'er-do-well, right? Never does a lick of work, either, unlike those he would have consider him their better."

"He's a snob, all right—and worse." In the face of O'Hare's steady gaze, Dorothea blushed again. "Jeremy Winton has always ordered me around as if I were his skivvy, me and the only other female at the paper, who works setting type. He's insulting, derogatory, and

23

suggestive. Today, though, he took it one step further."

"He propositioned you?"

"No, not quite." Dorothea gulped more cordial and shook her head; her hair slid down her back. "But he made it clear he expects me to accept advances from him if I want to keep my job."

"Mercy." O'Hare's gaze seemed to follow the trail Dorothea's hair took down her back, revisited her lips, and returned to her eyes. "The lout."

"Lout, yes. That's a perfect word for him. Also arrogant. He's an arrogant, supercilious bastard." She froze in horror. Had that last word really come out of her mouth? She might have thought it several times in relation to Jeremy Winton, but she'd never expected to say it aloud. The cordial seemed to be doing strange things to her indeed, but she did like the flavor.

O'Hare gave a small smile that put dimples into his cheeks. "So, bonny miss, what did you do?"

"I told him off royally. Informed him no one—no one!—treats Dorothea Sinclair like a lightskirt, that being a respectable woman I didn't deserve such treatment. And I threatened to report his behavior to his father if it continued."

"Ah. What did he say?"

Dorothea's anger rekindled. "He laughed at me. Laughed and scoffed. He told me to go ahead—he was surprised the old man hadn't already had me himself."

"The scoundrel."

"Indeed. He would not dare say such things were my father around." She inclined her head confidingly. "My father is the town blacksmith. As is my older brother. Well, he is not actually my brother, but more an honorary member of the family, and Jo's husband."

"That would be Jo your best friend, who features in your novel. Well, well—championed by a pair of blacksmiths! Enough to make any right-thinking man quake in his boots."

Dorothea narrowed her eyes. "Of course the Wintons don't know I'm championed by two blacksmiths."

"You didn't tell them?"

"Not in so many words, though I did imply I don't stand alone in the world. Just here, in Boston." For an instant she felt so bleak, she feared it showed.

"Look, Miss Dorothea—"

"It's Dora. My friends call me Dora." She emptied her glass and squinted at it.

"Dora, my darlin', if you'll take some more advice…"

"Certainly."

"Go home to your flanking blacksmiths before you come to some harm."

"I can't do that."

"It truly might be best."

"And admit defeat?"

"Look, from all I've heard, you have Jeremy Winton's measure right—he is a bad one, and he learned it all at his father's knee. Best to cut your losses and put the pair of them behind you."

"No, oh, no. There's a better way to get even with them."

Eunice bustled in and set two platters overflowing with food at their places. O'Hare waved his mug at the woman. "I'll have another, please."

"As will I." Dorothea lifted her glass.

Eunice gave O'Hare an inquiring look.

25

"I'm payin'," he said. "Bring her what she wants."

He pointed at Dorothea's plate. "Tuck in, now. Get a lining in your stomach before that second drink arrives."

"I will. It looks wonderful." Yet Dorothea paused with her fork aloft and stared at him owlishly. "You don't think I'm tipsy, do you?"

"On one cordial? Impossible."

"Impossible. You're right."

"I'm frequently right, darlin'. And when it comes to you returning home—"

"But no—listen to my idea first. It involves you."

"Don't tell me; you want to snag an interview with me."

"Did I already tell you?"

"More or less." He waved a hand. "But go ahead and expand on it."

"Expand—that's a very good word. It implies all kinds of open-ended possibilities."

"I'm all about possibilities, me."

"This beef is very good."

"Best in Boston."

She leaned still farther across the table and gazed into his eyes. "So, O'Hare, how would you like to make my byline the best in Boston?"

Chapter Four

"Well, now," O'Hare said, giving it due consideration, "that's an intriguing prospect."

"Isn't it?" Dorothea Sinclair tore her beautiful eyes from his and looked around the room. "Where's that woman with our drinks?"

"Never mind that, for the moment." O'Hare reached across the scarred table—it looked like someone had been playing knives for pints on its surface—and covered Dorothea's hand. "One thing at a time here, lass. Just exactly what are you asking of me?"

She blinked at their linked hands before raising those great, fey eyes to his. "Well, here it is: you could make my career by giving me an exclusive interview, and I believe I could further your cause with it."

"My cause?"

"Almost ever since I arrived here in Boston I've heard about you—the rebel Irishman who's determined to make things fair for the Irish here in Boston. But let me tell you, most of what I've heard has come from the mouths of your detractors. No one's got your side of it—from the horse's mouth, as it were."

"I see."

"You're considered a very nefarious man."

"Am I, then?"

"That means—"

"I know what it means; I may be Irish, but I'm not ignorant, though the toffs in this town seem to think it means one and the same."

"Well, but with such a reputation, people are going to believe the worst of you, even more so if you don't present your position in your own words. I'm offering you the opportunity to state your case, clear up some misunderstandings, and perhaps garner support. Your cause is just. You deserve a chance to define it."

"You consider my cause just, eh?"

"Well, of course—as just as is my own in refusing that pig's advances. Why should Irish workers be paid less for the same day's work? Why should they be charged more for housing? Why are they the first to be fired, and from the lowest-paying jobs? Irish girls cleaning English society women's privies. Irish lads made to run errands for less than a penny a day…"

"I know how it goes, miss." O'Hare had once been one of those lads and knew the sting of seeing his "betters" ride by in fine carriages behind their high-stepping horses as if he didn't exist. "They say we're good for nothing but drinking and fighting—with some whoring thrown in for good measure."

"Then set them straight. In your own words, in the *Guardian*."

O'Hare thought about it. "What's to make that bastard Winton print a true account of what I say? I doubt there's a hint of veracity in that rag of his."

Her gaze held his. "I'll tell him you've granted me an exclusive series of interviews—that you'll speak only to me and will break the whole thing off if he doesn't print the interview as I present it."

"Smart lass."

"He won't dare misrepresent you. And I'll do your story justice, you'll see. I'll even let you read the copy before I turn it in. Once the series starts running, there won't be a soul in Boston—rich or poor—but buys a paper. I'll be able to show what I'm made of and, incidentally, pay back that Jeremy Winton."

O'Hare narrowed his eyes. "It might indeed be an advantage for me to state my side of things." Better than that, it would give him an excuse to see Dorothea Sinclair again. A series of interviews, she said. That meant a series of meetings.

Fine, that. But would he be able to keep his hands off her? Either way, he wouldn't mind throwing a spanner in the works of that scunner Winton.

He smiled at her. "Finish your meal while I think about it. You can't expect a man to make such an important decision on the fly."

"By all means. But first, please find out what's become of my cherry cordial."

****

The music started up just as they finished their meal and decided to leave—a man with a squeaky fiddle and another with a squeeze box. A third kept time with a pair of spoons.

Dorothea would have lingered to listen, but the fight broke out only a minute later, when they were halfway across the tavern. Someone swore at the man next to him at the bar, someone else threw a punch, and suddenly blows rained from every side.

The fiddler stopped on the upbow. A table went over just behind Dorothea, and a body came flying in her direction.

Suddenly, as easy as nothing, she became airborne.

It took her an instant to grasp the fact that O'Hare's hands had closed around her waist, lifting her high off the floor while the brawler passed beneath her.

She gave an involuntary whoop as he swung her round, her feet still flailing, and carried her swiftly to a corner, out of the main line of fire.

"There now," he said and set her down slowly, his warm hands sliding upward from her waist over her ribs and stopping just beneath her bosom.

Dorothea froze. She could feel the heat from his hands on the undersides of both breasts, could feel the muscles rigid in his arms and see the light flare in his eyes. Suddenly, despite the chaos all around them, it felt as if the two of them stood alone—as if he might kiss her.

She wanted him to kiss her.

But no. This was the infamous O'Hare, a man she didn't know and dared not trust too far. She'd have to be mad to kiss him.

No one had ever called Dorothea Sinclair mad. Impractical, yes. Pig-headed, maybe. A bit too impulsive for her own good. But look where it had got her now.

Someone knocked her hat from behind, and it sailed into the midst of the fray.

"Ah, blast!" O'Hare exclaimed and waded in after it.

Dorothea stood clutching the edge of the overturned table behind which he'd deposited her and watched the swath he cut, marked by the banner of copper curls. He shoved a man here, pushed another there, knocked the heads of two combatants together, and disappeared briefly from view. When he came up again, he bore her hat in his hands.

He rejoined her an instant later, his eyes full of laughter. "A bit more battered than it was, I'm afraid. Let's get out of here."

"But how will we reach the door?"

In answer, he swept her up and bore her through the chaos; before she could blink twice, they slid out into the chilly night.

"I think it's safe for you to put me down now," Dorothea said.

"Eh?" Mere inches from hers, his gaze seemed to consume her. If anything, his arms tightened.

Temptation sizzled through Dorothea like hot fat on a griddle. She wanted to kiss him—oh, yes, wanted to know how those clever lips tasted and whether he'd melt her the way she suspected.

But he set her down on her feet and clamped the hat to her head. Amusement flooded his face.

"More trouble than it's worth, that hat—not but it is fetching."

"And, I fear, quite ruined," Dorothea lamented, striving to cover her discomfort. "But thank you anyway." She adjusted the hat. "What were they fighting about, do you know?"

"Someone wanted a certain song and someone else wanted a different one, from what I heard. Are you all right, though?"

"Yes, thanks to you."

He gave her a third bow. "Glad to be of service."

"And—?" Dorothea prompted.

"And?"

"Have you decided to take me up on my offer?"

"Offer?" His gaze inspected her lips, and heat

31

flooded through her yet again. Sharp and abrupt, she relived the feel of his hands beneath her breasts.

"The interviews. Will you do them?"

"Ah, well." For a moment he stared away into the night, and Dorothea held her breath. She wanted this opportunity. She wanted a chance to see him again.

"Let me get you home. I'll give you my answer then."

This time it felt right—and safe—to walk with her arm linked through his. He took her through streets she didn't recognize to a main thoroughfare she did and thence to the tall gray boarding house.

"I detest this place," she confessed reflexively.

O'Hare slanted a look at her. "Then move. There's a thousand other places to stay."

"This is respectable. Safe."

She drew her arm from his reluctantly and turned to face him.

"Thank you for your help this evening."

"You're welcome, Miss Sinclair."

"And may I have your answer?"

He mused, his eyes narrowed. "It's about taking chances, isn't it? You have to take one, and so do I. We have to gamble on each other."

"I guess you're right."

He leaned close. "Then yes, I'll take a chance on you, Dorothea Sinclair."

Her heart bounded. "Wonderful! When—?"

"I'll send word."

And before she could pin him down further, he strode away into the night.

Chapter Five

"Two more men let go at Whittaker's, and a whole slew dismissed from the dock at Southside. Good workers, too, and with families to support. The only reason we can see is that they'd been making their complaints known. One of them had gone to the foreman at Southside asking for a decent wage—as much as his non-Irish fellow workers earn—so he could feed his kiddies."

O'Hare blew out a breath and rubbed at his forehead, which had begun to ache. He'd come here, straight from his own job at the cabinetmaker's, to the stifling, tiny room at the top of this house where he and his cohorts met, because Riley said it was urgent.

He hated this place, which always felt airless and stuffy no matter the temperature outside. But it had yet to be discovered, and needs must.

He eyed Riley who, as usual, looked worried. A string bean of a man and what they called Black Irish, Riley had come from Ireland at the age of sixteen and bore the genuine accent O'Hare lacked.

No one among O'Hare's cohorts cared that he'd been born in America. His face declared him as Irish as any of them.

He gave a tight smile as he considered it. Here he was, leading the cause of the Irish in Boston, and him but half-blooded. When he'd asked his ma—pestered her about it, in fact—she'd admitted his father had been full-blood Irish and born on the old sod, though she'd failed to provide a name. But she was of Scottish descent.

And no better than she should be.

"Something will have to be done," he told Riley.

"I agree, but what?" Riley's gray eyes, which tended to reflect his emotions all too accurately, shone with distress. "We need something that will get us arrested."

"Do we?"

"Aye. 'Tis the only way we earn any real notice. And those men need their jobs back right quick."

"Have they gone and asked for them back?"

Riley scowled. "Two of them did, to no avail. The rest said they'd be damned if they'd crawl on their bellies to that lot o' muck."

"Sometimes we have to bend." O'Hare reflected upon it. "And sometimes we need to stay strong."

Riley took a swig from the pint of black ale at his elbow. "I say we need a grand gesture that will grab the notice of everyone in this city."

"And have them send the coppers in?" Last time they'd attempted a grand gesture—staged a strike of the dockworkers—the mayor had sent the cops to make wholesale arrests, and the court had supported him, sending down cruel and unreasonable sentences.

"We have to be more careful than that."

"Careful won't put food in the bellies o' those hungry bairns."

"So it won't. Organize the Irish shopkeepers—see if they're willing to extend some credit."

"They've already extended so much some of them

can't pay their suppliers. Hard to do business when your patrons are all out o' work."

"Perhaps it's time for a donation. I could go see Marielle again."

Now Riley grunted. "Careful with that. There's already plenty of talk about the two of you. You don't want to give her husband cause to cast her off—not because she should stay married to the beast but because that would cut off the flow of money, sure."

"So it would. But Dickenson will never cast her off. He's far too besotted."

And who wouldn't be? Marielle Dickenson might well be the bonniest woman O'Hare had ever seen. That was... A vision of tumbling black hair and fey eyes danced across his mind, and he hastily dismissed it.

Marielle's story was an unusual one. She'd stepped off a boat from Ireland as a girl and gone right into service. With a face like a flower, a mass of golden ringlets, and a generous figure, she'd soon caught the eye of her employer's son. But the girl, smart as well as beautiful, held out for marriage. Dickenson senior, a land developer, had wealth to burn and settled a great deal of it on his son.

Accepted into Boston society for the sake of her husband's position, Marielle had bloomed, taking on the airs, status, and wardrobe of a lady born. O'Hare knew, though, where her sympathies lay. They'd been friends from a young age, and he knew Marielle as hardheaded and true of heart. Her husband's money, channeled through her, had been spent to fill more than a few Irish bellies.

Yet as Riley pointed out, O'Hare couldn't expect to go to that well too often. And he had to remember the other danger that lay in Marielle's company…in his past feelings for her.

"I say we stage another demonstration," Riley proposed.

"Maybe. But not yet. Let me give it some thought." Dorothea Sinclair's face flashed before his eyes again. "I have something else on a string."

Yes, he'd promised to grant her interviews, and he liked to keep his word, mainly because he knew enough men who didn't. Would that work to his advantage? Would those interviews give them the splash they needed?

Before he could make up his mind, an urchin ran into the room.

"Hare O'Hare!" the lad cried, the name his familiars called him. O'Hare knew the boy and nearly groaned aloud. Not that. Not now.

But the lad, whose name was Sean, called out, "Mister Gene says you're to come and hurry. He says 'tis the end this time!"

Mister Gene—Eugene Browne, one of the men who very rarely kept his word, ever. O'Hare remained where he was, sprawled in his seat.

Riley raised a black eyebrow. "Are ye not going to go, lad? Sure, you know what this summons means."

"He's sent word it was the end before. She always rallies."

"Heartless!" Riley huffed. "'Tis your mother of whom we're speakin', lad."

"I know who she is."

He should. Maggie Grier Browne was the only parent he'd ever known. Past barmaid, past whore, she'd run away with Eugene Browne, a traveling salesman, when O'Hare was only three. The years since had proved turbulent. Even though she'd later married Browne, their relationship had not been what anyone could deem loving.

Yet they'd stayed together all this while. And now his mother, Maggie, hovered on the brink of death.

Or so Gene would have him think.

He looked Sean in the eye. "Did you see her, lad?"

Sean nodded vigorously. His face looked like a jug with ears for handles. "I did."

"And how did she look?"

"Like death, sor!"

That told O'Hare nothing. Lately Maggie always looked like death. The doctor said, though, she had something evil growing in her belly where O'Hare himself had begun life.

He sighed, and Riley gave him a push. "Go to her, you great lump."

Outside, rain spat from the direction of the ocean, and all the streetlamps wore haloes. O'Hare's Celtic blood sent a spear of cold up his spine. A night for ghosts, this. They might linger anywhere. Was it also a night for death to come?

He followed Sean through twisting streets to the poor tenement Eugene now called home. Sean lived on the ground floor with his ma, Gene and Maggie on the upper; the place reeked of boiled cabbage. O'Hare paused and peered into Sean's face.

"I don't suppose Mr. Gene paid you for his errand?"

"No, sor."

O'Hare pressed a penny into the lad's hand. "Run along inside."

"I can't, Mister Hare. Have to stand out front and watch for the banshee. Think she'll come?"

O'Hare experienced another cold tremor. "I very much doubt it. Go inside."

But the boy stood as if rooted, and O'Hare skipped up the dark, malodorous staircase, a hundred thoughts crowding his mind.

In how many such vile places had they lived over the years, while he grew? From how many had they been tossed by landlords tired of waiting for rent? Gene had been what O'Hare called an itinerant worker, never staying at one job long. A born salesman, he'd hawked any manner of things over the years, from get-rich-quick schemes to patent medicines. Eugene Browne talked a good game; he never followed through.

O'Hare reached the door and scratched on it, using the code they'd employed since his boyhood. Gene swung the panel wide.

"Thank God you've come."

Gene Browne looked like a man made of sticks tied together in loose bunches. He had a head of brown hair and a face gaunt as a skull, long arms and legs, big hands with skeletal fingers. His hazel eyes always looked hungry; now they looked despairing, as well, and O'Hare experienced a qualm. Could this really be the end?

"Come in, boy, come in. She's bad, right bad. And asking for you."

O'Hare's brows flew up. His mother never asked for him. Rather, she'd spent most of his life wishing him elsewhere.

"Has the doc been?"

Gene looked uneasy. "No money for the doc. But

I'll send for him now, if—?"

Ah, so that was it: Gene wanted money. Again. This summons was just a ploy to get it.

But Gene tossed his head. "I don't doubt it's too late for the doc, anyway. I think she's goin' this time."

Leaving his stepfather, O'Hare walked through the poorly lit room to the little closet of a bedroom beyond. There a single lamp burned and illuminated the woman in the bed.

Maggie Grier Browne might have been comely once. She'd certainly shared her favors, and few men had turned her down. Now her once-auburn hair had faded to gray and needed to be combed. Her skin had a gray hue, also, and the smell in the room rocked O'Hare back on his heels. Only her eyes looked the same: they reached for him as he stepped in.

"Timmy. You came."

No one called him Timmy anymore. Only this woman, and that seldom enough.

"Ma."

"I wanted to see you, wanted to tell—"

A spasm took her, made her double her arms over her stomach and grimace. O'Hare stood by the side of the bed and watched. When it passed she reached for his wrist.

"Sit. I don't think I have much time."

Suddenly, O'Hare believed it. The look in her eyes convinced him.

He perched on the edge of her bed reluctantly. It had been years since he'd been this close to her. Maggie had never been the sort of mother to shower her son with affection.

And what did he see in her face now? Pain,

determination, and something he'd never beheld there before. Wistfulness?

She smelled of whiskey, and a half-filled glass stood on the bedside table. Drink had featured prominently in her life ever since O'Hare could remember.

Her voice came in a rasp. She followed his gaze and nodded at the glass. "Gene has been keeping me dosed—against the pain. It's bad. But that doesn't matter. Won't be long now."

"If you want money for the doctor—"

"Is that why you think I sent for you? Money?"

O'Hare answered honestly, "It usually is."

A ghostly smile crossed her face. "Fair is fair, son. I fed you all those years. You wouldn't warrant what I had to do in the beginning, to keep your gob full. Men with their paws all over me. Now you have a steady job, it's only right you pay me back."

"Jesus," O'Hare said under his breath.

Her eyes flashed. "Can't deny I raised you up."

O'Hare's lips twisted. "Can't deny that."

"But I never told you everything. You must have wondered. Your father…"

Another spasm hit her, and she broke off. O'Hare could feel Gene hovering in the doorway behind him and wanted to tell the bastard to bugger off.

But it was Gene who stepped forward and tipped the whiskey to his wife's lips.

"There now, Maggie."

Tenderness? Surely not. There'd been a lot between these two—never that.

Maggie gulped and grimaced. Finally she resumed, "I want to give you your father's name—while I still can. Come closer."

O'Hare leaned in. The sharp scent of cheap Irish couldn't cover another, fouler smell.

Maggie stared into his eyes. "Declan O'Shea—that was your father's name. Why did you never make me tell you that?"

O'Hare shrugged.

"You thought I didn't know his name," she guessed. "But I did. He was a right rascal, born, as I told you before, in the old sod and with the blarney to prove it. Well, you can tell that—just look at you. You're the spit of him. The spit."

O'Shea, O'Hare thought. Well, hell.

"He was another woman's husband when he got you on me—a liar and a cheat. I don't want you to be ashamed of that."

"No?"

"He was what he was."

"And how does he make his living, this paragon?"

"Lobster fisherman, back in Maine—though he never devoted much effort to it. He always spent his time tipping a pint—or a woman. He liked chasing a woman better than the actual act, I think."

Patter—Gene had a line of patter, too. Maggie must have a weakness for it.

"Where is he now? Back in Maine?" And if he were, would O'Hare go look him up? Tell him, "Look me in the face and guess who I am."

But Maggie said, "Dead. He died the same year you were born. But you have a half-brother there—Douglas Grier. And no doubt a litter of nieces and nephews; I heard he married." She gave a ghastly smile. "Oh, yes, I sought news of him, though you and he

41

might not warrant it."

"So, Ma, why tell me all this now?"

"Because I may not be able to tell you tomorrow. This is it, son." To his surprise she reached out and took his hand. "A man has a right to know where he came from, no matter how ugly the story."

A cheat and a liar knocking up a barmaid—no, O'Hare couldn't be proud of that. Yet he had a name now for the Irish blood that more or less defined him. O'Shea.

His mother's fingers tightened. "I'm proud of you, Timmy. That's what I wanted to say. You didn't turn out like him. Or me—or Gene, for all that. There's something fine and steady in you. Not sure how that happened."

Neither was O'Hare, but unexpected tears stung his eyes. He would not weep for this woman who had never shed a tear over him.

"So," she sighed and sank back into the pillow, looking suddenly frail. "Maybe I did one good thing in this world."

Chapter Six

O'Hare extracted a bill from his wallet and offered it to Gene. "Go get her some opium for the pain. I know you've given it to her before. Is this enough?"

Gene licked his lips, and his gaze moved back to O'Hare's wallet. "She'll need some more whiskey, too."

"No, she won't."

"I'll need it." Gene's mud-colored eyes met O'Hare's. "If I lose her, boy—how will I go on? Have some pity on me. I've been like a father to you."

"You have not."

"Raised you from the age of three."

Yes, if anyone decent could call it raising. The man had given him house room—when they had a house. But O'Hare wouldn't argue it now. He feared Gene might start blubbing, a prospect so terrible it defied imagination.

He withdrew another bill. "Something for yourself, then."

Gene's face lit greedily. "Bless you, boy. You've turned out good, like she says." He hesitated. "Will you wait till I get back? I wouldn't like her to pass alone."

O'Hare glanced toward the other room. Suddenly he didn't want to go back in there and face the wasted woman who was his mother.

"Be quick," he told Gene.

Gene loped off, and O'Hare crossed to the room's single window and watched him. Black as pitch outside and as dreary a night as the month of May ever produced.

He wondered if Sean still waited below, watching for the banshee, and told himself not to be so fanciful. Yet his Irish blood was up, and his skin pricked all over his body.

Irish blood. So—his father truly had been full-blooded Irish, right from the sod. O'Shea. No one who looked at him would ever doubt it, yet the knowledge added steel to the cause O'Hare now fought.

Blood will out, so people said. He knew Maggie's parents—now long dead—had come from Ayr in Scotland as newlyweds and fallen on hard times. That made O'Hare all Celt, but with roots torn up and very nearly without family.

Except a half-brother somewhere in Maine. Douglas. Douglas Grier.

He wondered why Maggie had left Douglas behind when she ran off with Gene; he'd just decided to go into the bedroom and ask her when he saw something in the glass.

No—it was the reflection of something. For he could dimly see himself mirrored in the smudged, dirty pane, and behind his shoulder, in the doorway of the bedroom, a figure all in white.

It looked like his ma. How had she found the strength to get up out of her bed? He whirled around and saw no one standing in the room—just the empty bedroom doorway.

He knew then, but went into the bedroom anyway, to find her lying with her head cocked on the pillow, her mouth gaping open and both palms turned upward on the blanket as if she pled for something.

Release, maybe. And so the angel of death had come—no banshee, just a stroke of mercy at the end.

"Oh, Ma," he whispered.

She, of course, made no reply, even though her eyes, still open, stared right at him.

He closed them gently and folded her hands together.

Gone, gone, gone, and with her a big lump of his life.

He sank to the edge of the bed and covered his face with his hands.

****

"Be a darling and bring me some tea, do." Jeremy Winton delivered the request as he passed Dorothea's desk on the way to his father's office.

She looked up at him, iron in her backbone and steel in her gaze. "I'm sorry, Mr. Winton, but I won't."

"What?" His step faltered, and he looked back at her. For an instant their gazes clashed and tangled; he returned to her desk.

"I thought we had this out the other night."

"So did I. You behaved most improperly toward me."

He stepped closer—too close for Dorothea's comfort—and lowered his voice even though the noise in the big room precluded anyone overhearing. They did attract several interested glances but no more.

Jeremy Winton stood about five foot ten and dressed like a dandy, his cuffs snowy white, his suit the latest fashion. The fact that he had a face like a ferret somewhat ruined the splendid effect. Since his father looked like an aged ferret, Dorothea figured Jeremy couldn't help it if he made her skin crawl.

Somehow she found the courage to hold his gaze. His eyes, pale blue, had pupils like pinpricks.

He said, "You will provide me with tea or whatever else I request."

Dorothea pushed to her feet; she didn't like him looking down at her. "Mr. Winton, it seems you failed to get the message last time we spoke. I'm an employee here, not your personal servant."

His nostrils flared. "It's you who failed to get the message, sweetheart. You're whatever I say you are—that is, if you want to keep your job." He quirked an eyebrow. "Perhaps you're not aware you actually owe your job here to me."

"How is that?"

"I'm the one who encouraged my father to get with the times and hire some female employees." His gaze flicked her up and down. "Someone pretty, I told him. I must say he surpassed himself."

Dorothea said nothing, but heat climbed into her cheeks.

Winton leaned closer. "At the moment, however, you're flirting with dismissal. Are you truly so stupid you think we keep you here for your journalistic skills?"

Dorothea stiffened further and sucked in a breath.

"I'll tell you, Dorothea, aspiring reporters are thick on the ground in this city. We could replace you tomorrow—with a female willing to do anything to keep her post."

Dorothea hissed between her teeth, "You're disgusting."

"And you're far too attractive to be wasted scribbling down accounts of the ladies' historical society meeting. Now, how about that tea?"

"I'm afraid you'll have to get it yourself…sir."

Winton grunted. "Pack up your things. You're done here."

"Begging your pardon, Mr. Winton—I don't think you have the authority to dismiss me. Only your father can do that."

Steam virtually came out of Jeremy's ears. "Then give me five minutes."

He crashed into his father's office and closed the door with a bang. Several people close by stared at Dorothea. She could see her friend Molly Carter through the big windows of the typesetting room. Before Dorothea could collect her composure, Molly popped out and hurried to her desk.

Molly had shrewd blue eyes and fair hair gathered into a haphazard bun. With skin like cream, she might have claimed the title of beauty had she taken the least bit of trouble with her appearance. She didn't, but dressed in plain brown clothing that always looked like an afterthought. At the moment, she also wore a long, leather apron that protected her blouse and skirt against ink stains.

"What just happened?" she asked worriedly.

"Ferret-face tried to dismiss me."

Molly breathed a word no gently raised woman should know. "You don't say!"

"I do. Told me to pack up my things."

"I judge from that glint in your eye you mean to fight."

"Oh, you have no idea." Dorothea hadn't told

Molly about her encounter with O'Hare. So far, she'd told no one.

"The man's a walking scandal. Did you hear the latest? They say he beat up a whore the other night. Put her in hospital."

"He visits whores?" Dorothea's eyes narrowed.

Molly snorted. "The lads in there"—she jerked her head toward the typesetting room—"say he'll take it wherever he can get it."

"But that's assault. How is it he's not behind bars?"

"With all the power of Daddy's money behind him? Are you serious?"

Molly glanced at the window of Winton's office, behind which Jeremy could be seen posturing and waving his arms.

"Sure hope you don't get dismissed, Dora," she said. "I'd hate to be the only woman left here."

"Don't worry. I've a rabbit up my sleeve." Or, rather, a Hare. "You'd better get back to work before he sees you."

Molly snorted again but went. For all her boldness, she never forgot she had an ailing younger brother to support and couldn't afford to lose her job.

Well, and neither could Dorothea. If she lost this position and failed to find another, she'd have no choice but to go slinking back home with her tail between her legs. And while she adored her family, she didn't want to return to Maine under those conditions.

That thought stiffened her backbone and let her meet Jeremy's gaze when he swept out of the inner office, gave her a significant look, and gestured. "My father will see you now."

Dorothea entered the inner sanctum even as Jeremy left the newspaper office. Montgomery Winton greeted her with a cool stare meant to unnerve her. This encounter would not prove easy; Winton lived his life intimidating others and had made Dorothea uneasy from their very first meeting. She usually had strong instincts about people, and she didn't trust Montgomery or his son.

But she needed this position. Now to convince him he needed to keep her in it.

"Sit down," he barked.

She chose the chair that faced his desk, and he spent several moments applying himself to the papers that lay on its surface, a tactic meant to make her sweat.

At last he lifted his gaze to her.

"I told you when I hired you that this was a trial position. Your letter of application was very persuasive, and my son convinced me that in order to move with the times we needed more diversity in the office. As I recall, Miss Sinclair, at the time you expressed your gratitude most vociferously."

"Yes, sir, I did." She'd been unable to believe her good fortune. A position at a Boston newspaper—not the foremost or even a particularly well-respected one, but a newspaper all the same. Sure, she'd heard the *Guardian* described as everything from a rag to a scandal sheet. She hadn't cared.

Montgomery Winton stared at her down his ferret-like nose. "You, Miss Sinclair, swore your willingness to accept any assignment here in order to work your way up."

So she had.

"That, Miss Sinclair, includes fetching tea when

one of the owners requests it."

Owner? Was Jeremy Winton that? Dorothea shifted uneasily. "Are you referring, sir, to the incident a few minutes ago, or that which took place the other evening?"

"Both."

"Then I regret to inform you that the other night Mr. Jeremy Winton requested far more from me than tea. In fact"—her telltale cheeks once more heated—"he made a suggestion—no, more of a demand—to which no respectable woman should be subjected. I, Mr. Winton, am a respectable woman, and I'm sure you—"

"I don't care," Winton barked.

"I beg your pardon?"

"Miss Sinclair, I thought you understood the parameters of the employment offer I made you. You have joined the ranks of the newspaper world—a dog-eat-dog environment. Do you not think there are a hundred other young women who would appreciate the opportunity you've been given?"

"I suppose there are, Mr. Winton."

"And who would do anything to keep their positions?"

Dorothea's cheeks flared, along with her anger. Her mother often cautioned her about her hasty temper, to which she had to admit. It frequently escaped her control, especially under the impetus of indignation.

"Are you telling me I must submit to your son's sexual demands in order to keep my job?"

"Hundreds would."

"I am not *hundreds.*"

"Then, Miss Sinclair, I will have to ask you to clear

your desk. You'll be escorted from the office."

Dorothea surged to her feet. "I don't think so."

His brows flew up. "What did you say to me?"

She planted both hands flat on his desk and leaned toward him. "I came to Boston to be a reporter, Mr. Winton. Not a skivvy, not a servant, and certainly not an on-demand whore. I've spent the last three months fetching tea and proofing copy far inferior to my own, while avoiding your son's lecherous advances. This is not acceptable."

"You're right, it isn't. Get out of my sight."

"I don't think so."

"Leave before I summon the police."

"Mr. Winton, when I first came here, you made me an offer—a very poor offer, as it turned out. I'm about to give you a better one." Her eyes glinted as she went on. "I am a reporter, and I'll prove it by getting the *Guardian* an exclusive with one of the most notorious men in this city."

"What?"

"I'm offering you a series of interviews with O'Hare."

Mr. Winton's eyes narrowed. "You're mad. Every reporter in this city has been angling for an interview with him."

"I know."

"How would someone like you snag such a prize? He invariably refuses."

"Well, he hasn't this time. He's agreed to talk to me. But only to me."

Winton laughed incredulously. "How would you even gain access to such a man?"

"My methods are my own. But I can guarantee you

a series of interviews that will sell more papers than the *Herald* and the *Courier* combined."

"How many interviews?"

"Yet to be decided. But I get the byline."

He snorted. "You couldn't do the pieces justice."

"Just try me." Dorothea shrugged a shoulder. "Or don't. I'll take my exclusive to the *Herald*."

For the space of twenty heartbeats, Winton's gaze held Dorothea's. Then the newspaper magnate blinked.

"Bring me the first piece. We'll decide then whether you'll keep your job."

Dorothea exhaled a long breath. All she had to do now was locate O'Hare and hold him to his promise.

Chapter Seven

"Good morning, Marielle."

The woman on the dainty white mare drew up her mount, when O'Hare spoke, and bent her graceful neck. A smile curved lips as pink as rose petals, and O'Hare grinned in appreciation.

Ah, what a picture she made, lit by the clear, early light, her fair hair piled beneath a clever wee hat. Many a wealthy woman rode on Boston Common in the morning hours—he'd warrant none could match Marielle Dickenson.

Maisie, her name had originally been—Maisie O'Halloran, when she stepped off the boat from Ireland. Just like him, she'd altered it, deeming that name too common, but the charming Irish brogue remained.

It warmed her voice now when she said, "Hare O'Hare, as I live and breathe. To what do I owe this great honor?"

"Faith, you're as bonny as the morning."

She tossed her head. "It is a lovely morning, isn't it? But, me fine bucko, shouldn't you be spending it at work?"

"I just came from work. Walked all the way here to see you."

Her face sobered abruptly. "I heard about your ma, lad. I'm so sorry."

"She wasn't much of a mother."

"But she was all you had—and better than meself, cast on a strange shore with nary a relation to hand."

O'Hare let his gaze travel over her slowly and with appreciation. "You've done all right."

"I have, by the grace of God. So what does bring you to see me?"

"I need a word. And a favor."

She gave him a thoughtful look before deciding, "Let's walk." Raising an exquisitely gloved hand, she summoned a servant—a young lad in her train—who came at a run to help her dismount from the mare. She placed the reins in the young man's keeping.

"Walk her for me, Jack."

The lad nodded. About fifteen, he wore a neat uniform and looked nearly as Irish as O'Hare. Marielle made sure only Irish came to work in her husband's big mansion—and the places were good ones.

"Now then." She looped her arm through O'Hare's even as the boy led the horse away. "We'll enjoy the morning. So you haven't come just to catch up on old times."

"I have not, no," O'Hare admitted with regret even as they matched their steps and started off on a promenade.

"I haven't forgotten my origins, you know, even though I'm mistress of the big house instead of skivvy. Remember that awful winter when all we did was shovel snow?"

"How could I forget?" His fingers had turned blue and stayed that way for weeks.

"And how cold it was up in the attics where we slept! Not a lick o' heat. We maids huddled together all in the one bed in an effort to get warm." She slanted a look at him. "'Tisn't that way in Mr. Dickenson's house, I'll have you know. All my folk have decent rooms that are kept heated."

Did she realize she called her husband Mr. Dickenson? It denoted a certain distance between them. He wondered if it persisted when they were in bed at night.

"It was a miserly household, for certain." As a runner, or errand boy, O'Hare had been entitled to meals during the day, often the only ones he got if Gene happened to be out of work. "And a hungry one."

"Oh, yes." She pressed closer to his side. "Remember the time Cook passed out biscuits in a fit of pity, but I wasn't there—answering some call of our benighted mistress, I was. And you saved yours and gave it to me later?" Tears flooded her lovely blue eyes. "I'll never forget, never. 'Twas all I had to eat that day."

O'Hare said nothing but squeezed her arm comfortingly. He'd been a little bit in love with her then and would have given her anything. But she'd never seen him as anything more than a brother.

"And," she went on, "that time you were knocked down in the street by that carriage—they carried you back to the house, and Master said to put you out in the garden like a stray cat. He'd be damned if he'd waste doctor's fees on an *Irish* boy."

She stiffened with indignation, and O'Hare paused their steps. "We're still fighting that injustice, Marielle. Have you heard what's happened at the docks? A slew of Irish dismissed because they dared ask for enough money to feed their children. Not safer conditions, mind—even though two or three men take injuries there every day. Just last week, a cable broke, and a man was hurt so severely he may never walk again. What's to happen to his hungry children, eh?"

Compassion flooded Marielle's eyes. "You want money."

With a rueful smile, he admitted, "I do. I hate to go to the well too often. You've been wondrously generous. We're fighting for the kind of change that will make a real difference. But it's slow in coming, and meanwhile those families need a measure of compensation."

She sighed. "I'll see what I can do. Mr. Dickenson gives me a generous clothing allowance. If I forego a new gown for the May dance, I should be able to slip you something."

"Bless you, Marielle."

A mischievous smile played about her lips, and she leaned closer. "Bless you, *Timmy*."

"Och, don't call me that."

"So long as you know my true name, I can revel in knowing yours. What would your many detractors say, eh, if they knew the sweet name your ma called you?"

"I dread to think."

She measured him with her gaze. "For you have grown into a fine man, haven't you? A force to be reckoned with—infamous."

"And about to become more so. Keep watching the *Guardian*, lass. You may see news of me."

She wrinkled her nose. "That rag?"

"An opportunity's an opportunity."

"And you were ever one to make the most of those. I tell you, you should let me usher you into polite society. You'd cause ever such a sensation."

"The company I've been keeping is polite enough, thanks."

"But all cleaned up and put in a fine suit, you'd make the women swoon. I can't imagine, for all that, why some clever lass hasn't trapped you yet."

Clever lass. He thought again of Dorothea Sinclair—Dora. He liked the idea of calling her that. Impatience rolled through him. When would he see her again?

"And what does that look in your eyes mean, I wonder?"

"Naught."

"I don't believe you. Tell me, is there someone?"

"As if I have time for all that nonsense. I'm a busy man, you know. Ron and I are fitting a whole set of new cabinets in Mrs. Tyler's kitchen. And that's in addition to my other activities."

"Mrs. Tyler's? That's rarified air, indeed!"

"Those big jobs are the ones that pay." Some day he hoped to be half-owner in Ron Murray's cabinet company. For now, it was good steady work and skilled labor that brought him satisfaction. "Speaking of which, I'd better get back. Thank you, Marielle. You've been generous, as always."

"You'll have the money tomorrow. Meanwhile, I'd like to attend your ma's funeral."

Shocking that would be—the high society lady at the burial of a riddled slag.

He shook his head. "Thank you, lass, but it's already done. We planted her yesterday afternoon."

"Ah. And I suppose you paid for the coffin and all. That no-good stepfather of yours never did."

"True. But he insisted on flowers." One raggedy

bunch, over which Gene had fretted. "And he cried copious amounts of tears, so I reckon that makes up for it. Say what you will of him, Marielle, he loved her all those years."

"Aye. Aye, lad, and I suppose that's all any of us can hope for, in the end."

Chapter Eight

The message came soon after Dorothea arrived at the newspaper office, brought by a freckle-faced lad in a cloth cap. Dorothea unfolded the paper and read the message written in a bold, black hand.

Meet me at Sybil's Tea Room at four o'clock.

No signature—just the caricature of a large rabbit. No, a hare.

Dorothea's pulse leaped. She refolded the note and slid it into the front of her blouse. So—he did mean to keep his word.

As soon as she could manage it, she cornered Molly alone. "Listen, have you ever heard of a place called Sybil's Tea Room?"

Molly gave her a stare. "Surely you're not thinking of going there?"

"Why not?"

"The woman who runs it has a reputation. It's said she can put curses on people."

"Sounds interesting. Maybe there's a story in it."

"Maybe there is, at that. Your big breakthrough?"

"I hope so. How do I get to the place?"

Molly gave her directions and offered, "Would you like me to come with you? Might be safest."

Dorothea shook her head. The interviews with O'Hare had to be kept secret even from Molly, at least till the story broke. "Sybil's isn't in a real bad neighborhood, is it?"

"No, it's one of those borderline districts. Working women patronize the place—and Bohemian types."

"I wouldn't mind being a Bohemian type."

Molly grinned. "Nor I. That's a good idea, though, writing stories about the colorful areas of the city, the places the female readership might not ordinarily see."

"Oh, I think so," Dorothea replied.

****

She went directly from the newspaper office later that day, her spine rigid with determination and her stomach doing somersaults. She couldn't dwell on how much depended on this encounter. Nor could she admit, even to herself, half her roiled emotions stemmed from anticipation. She wanted to see O'Hare again.

Wanted it badly.

She'd dressed soberly that morning in a brown skirt and jacket, white blouse, and small brown hat. The blue hat O'Hare had rescued still needed some serious repair before she could wear it again.

She splurged on a cab, which dropped her off in a narrow street full of shops and busy pedestrians. The patrons entering and exiting Sybil's seemed to be a mixture of working-class matrons and the Bohemians Molly had mentioned. Dorothea looked as out of place as a brown hen among peacocks.

Inside, Sybil's proved to be a dark, narrow shop with beads hanging in the window. Ignoring a frisson of uneasiness, Dorothea surveyed the place. Tables all draped in scarves of varying hues crowded the space, most of them occupied. Groups of women and a few men conversed earnestly, while one or two servers, dressed in midnight blue, glided about like ships in full sail. In one corner, a young woman played a viola, the music a thin backdrop for all the voices.

She would love to write a color piece about the place, but she hadn't come for that, not now.

She couldn't see O'Hare anywhere. Maybe he had yet to arrive. She decided to sit at a table, if she could find one, and order tea to steady her nerves.

Before she'd taken five steps, a woman issued from behind the counter that stretched across the rear of the shop and made for Dorothea. Tall and built to statuesque proportions, she had ink-black hair, worn in a chignon, and she trailed scarves the way a steamship did banners.

"Miss Sinclair?" she inquired in a spectral whisper. "Come with me."

They wound their way through the maze of tables to the back, where Dorothea saw the long counter had glass panels beneath and was filled with exquisite creations—small iced cakes and crème horns, cream puffs, and Napoleons. Before she could do more than begin to admire, her guide swept her past the counter and through a highly varnished door to where all the noise fell away.

The woman fixed her with a brilliant, dark stare. "You are here to meet Hare?"

"O'Hare, yes."

"He is called Hare O'Hare—the one who flees quickly, the clever changer."

"I beg your pardon?"

"Sybil sees and knows many things. You have an interesting aura. You must let me do a reading some time."

"I—"

"In there." Sybil gestured to yet another door.

Cautiously, Dorothea pushed it open and stepped in. A wave of scent met her—heavy patchouli mixed with incense. The place must be Sybil's private room, for scarves and cloths woven with strange symbols covered every surface including the table where O'Hare sat at his apparent ease.

He shot to his feet when he saw Dorothea, and their eyes met. A slow thrill chased its way down Dorothea's spine, very like the onset of fever. In the light cast by the overhead lamp, his copper curls gleamed with warmth; his eyes were those of a cat.

Dorothea thought suddenly of her friend Jo's cat back home, a big, orange tom, with similar eyes, who stalked through the world with supreme confidence.

"I've never liked that cat," Dorothea's mother always said. "Reminds me of someone…"

She wondered if her mother would like O'Hare, and then he smiled at her, and she forgot everything else—even, for the moment, her reason for being here.

"Good afternoon, Miss Sinclair."

"Afternoon, O'Hare. Or is it Hare O'Hare, as our hostess says?"

"I'd be pleased if you'd call me Hare. Will you sit down?"

He held the chair for her like the gentleman he might or might not be. She ran a quick eye over him as he joined her at the table. Today he had neglected the long leather coat and wore a workman's clothing— short woolen jacket with heavy breeches. But the shirt beneath, deep green, brightened the color in his eyes by contrast.

Responding to her close inspection, he said,

"Forgive my appearance. I came straight from the job."

"Where do you work?"

"I'm a woodworker. Cabinetmaking."

"A skilled trade."

"Yes. My employer, Ron Murray, is a true craftsman and caters to the wealthiest homeowners in this city."

"Did you apprentice to him?" Dorothea smiled. "My father took a young lad as apprentice, back before I was born. He's the one I mentioned—like an older brother to me."

"You said his wife's your best friend. No, I didn't 'prentice to Ron, at least not officially. He caught me stealing from him one afternoon and asked me why. I told him I hadn't eaten in two days." Hare smiled. "It was a lie—I hadn't eaten in three. Instead of turning me in to the coppers, he gave me a meal. I started hanging around after that, mostly hoping for another feed. Curious, I watched how he did things in the shop, and eventually took to it. Ron insists I have a natural talent."

He cocked an eyebrow at her. "You, Miss Sinclair, must have a prodigious memory. Aren't you going to write all this down? For your story, I mean. The infamous O'Hare and his humble beginnings…"

"I do have a prodigious memory, as a matter of fact. But this is your chance to tell me what you wish. I promised you'd get to tell your side of things. That can go any way you wish—human interest, angry diatribe, soapbox, heated defense. I want to put you in the very best light."

"Why? You barely know me. Why should you care what the good people of Boston think of me?"

"Well, you did come to my rescue. And you're giving me this opportunity. Reporters are supposed to be impartial, and when I get to the writing portion of this, I will be. For now—sway me, convince me." Charm me, she added silently. It likely wouldn't take much—a couple more of those slightly wicked smiles, another stare from between those copper lashes, and she might melt like harbor ice in spring.

"Why don't we start with a cup of tea? And some of Sybil's magnificent pastries."

Their hostess materialized at the door of the room as if by magic.

"Two cuppas please, Syb," Hare requested. "And a wee plate of your best."

"Who is she?" Dorothea asked when the woman went out. "A seer? A gypsy?"

"A little bit both, I think. She told me she comes from Vienna. And she's made some amazing predictions. Who can say?"

Sybil soon returned, bearing a tray piled high with a tea service and a tempting selection of pastries like those Dorothea had seen in the glass case.

"Oh, my," Dorothea exclaimed. "I feel like a princess."

In her spectral voice Sybil declared, "Every woman should feel like royalty from time to time."

She swept out, and Hare laughed softly. "You're afraid of her, Miss Dorothea."

"I am not."

"You are. Just look at your face."

"Well, you must admit she has a forbidding aspect. Does she make these delicacies herself?" Dorothea chose a tiny layer cake and bit into it. "Ah, wonderful!"

"She claims she makes them all herself. Personally, I think there's a crew of elves in the kitchen. If she ever thanks them, the magic stops."

"I hope she never thanks them, then. That's one of the best things I've ever tasted."

"Have another."

"You always seem to feed me when we meet."

"Food brings people together—as, unfortunately, does the lack of it. Shall we start our interview there, Miss Dorothea? With how many children go to bed hungry in this city and what proportion of them are Irish?"

For the next hour he spoke unhurriedly while Dorothea listened with avid attention and, thinking better of trusting her memory completely, pulled a notebook from her pocket and made copious notations. The tea went cold and the pastries were forgotten as she fell into the mind of the man opposite her.

A good mind, an intelligent one, she realized, his arguments well-reasoned—tough yet compassionate. Her respect for him rose as the minutes flowed by, along with her admiration.

None of the terrible things she'd heard about him seemed to fit. Dangerous, they called him—ruthless and cunning. He wanted to tear down the rules of society and rip the city apart at the seams.

She didn't see it. He detested injustice, yes, and noticed it all around him. To him, class represented an abominable divide that needed to be abolished.

She couldn't say she disagreed with that.

At last she laid down her pen and stretched cramped fingers.

He nodded at the pad. Throughout their time

together he'd remained lounging in his chair, the words just streaming from him with no seeming effort. Oh, for the gift of the blarney!

And was everything he'd told her the truth? She thought so.

"You've a lot of information there. I wonder what you'll make of it."

"I'll write something up tonight. Would you like to see it before I submit it to my editor?"

He shook his head. "I trust you, Dorothea Sinclair. What did the fine Montgomery Winton say then, when you presented your scheme?"

"He's avid for the series, as I knew he'd be."

"You just make sure he deals fairly with you, now. And that you get your byline." He grinned. "Him, I don't trust."

"Nor do I." She leaned toward him across the table. "I'm going to make a hero of you, Hare O'Hare. A bloody, first-class hero."

Chapter Nine

Two days later, Hare picked up a copy of the *Guardian* on his way to the cabinet shop when he heard the hawker shout, "Read about the hero of south Boston! Get it here, first in a series!"

The boy stared at O'Hare and, when he tried to pay him, grinned. "Complimentary copy to you, sor!"

O'Hare arrived at the cabinet shop to find Ron with the *Guardian* spread out on the main workbench, already reading.

He looked up. "You're famous, son. But who's this reporter—D. R. Sinclair?"

"Is that what she put?" O'Hare hurried to look at the sheet over which Ron had been poring. Clever girl.

"She?" Ron gave him a doubtful look. "A female reporter wrote this?"

"Yes." O'Hare swept the article, placed prominently on the front page. "In-depth series," he read and then the actual title of the article, "A Hungry Heart." Ah—so that was the direction she'd taken.

Ron pushed the lamp closer. "Here, read."

"But we've a load of work on."

"Nothing that can't wait."

O'Hare pored over the article, soon becoming lost in the tale D. R. Sinclair had written—that of a disadvantaged young boy, just one among many, hungry for far more than food to fill his belly, ravenous for justice, fairness, and an equal chance in life.

The fight O'Hare leads, she wrote at the end, *is a fight for survival. And what won't a hungry child do, to survive?*

He stood stunned for a full minute, when he finished, before he said, "Is this supposed to be about me?"

"It certainly is. He—or, so you say, she—has reached right out and snared her readers' hearts. No one, lad, will ever look at you the same. Nor will they look at a hungry Irish child the same, I dare say." Ron squeezed Hare's shoulder. "I'm proud of you."

"Better to be proud of her. I'm amazed Winton printed this." O'Hare tapped the paper with his finger. "It flies in the face of the hard line he usually takes."

"He's probably afraid to cross Miss D. R. Sinclair. Supposed to be a series, right? What's to stop her taking the next story to the *Herald*?"

"But newspapers don't print this kind of thing."

"They do now, lad. They do now."

****

"We sold out of papers by eleven a.m. and had to run a second edition," Montgomery Winton said in satisfaction. "It's even selling on the south side— especially on the south side."

His son Jeremy made a face and glared at Dorothea, who stood in Winton's office, her hands folded. "D. R. Sinclair. Were you ashamed to use your name and admit you're a woman?"

"Far from it. Reporters often use their initials. Besides, that is my name."

"It implies you're male."

"I don't think so. Most reporters in this city are

male, so people may assume it. I'm not responsible for their assumptions."

"And," Jeremy continued as if she hadn't spoken, "it's bad writing. This article is slanted. You've made a hero of an ignorant Irish troublemaker."

Dorothea's cheeks flushed with outrage. Before she could speak, Montgomery Winton did. "You're wrong, Jeremy. It's bloody brilliant writing. It's a color piece, not straight reporting. Besides," he admitted comfortably, "everything in the *Guardian* is slightly slanted. We have our own viewpoint."

"It isn't just that. She's glorified a man who's been arrested—how many times?"

As coolly as she could manage, Dorothea said, "I mean to take up his career campaigning for Irish rights in a future article. And begging your pardon, Mr. Winton"—she fixed Jeremy with a fierce stare—"you are not in a position to judge whether what I've written about O'Hare is true. You weren't there for the interview. I was."

"How many stories do you plan?" Winton the elder asked her.

"At least three."

"Make it six. We'll run one a week to keep interest up, just like the old fiction serials."

"It is fiction, most of it," Jeremy scoffed. " 'A Hungry Heart.' Even the title's sympathetic."

"She's pulled at her readers' heartstrings, and there's nothing wrong with that so long as those are attached to their purse strings. I'm in this business to make money—and outsell my competitors. I'll take any damned tone I have to, to accomplish that."

When Jeremy said nothing, Winton fixed Dorothea

with a stare. "Curiosity about your identity is already high. We've had several inquiries from the *Courier* and the *Herald*, fishing for information. No one knows you're a woman. Let's keep it that way for now."

"All right," Dorothea agreed slowly.

"But I want your promise you won't take the balance of this series to one of my competitors."

"I have no intention of doing so, sir, so long as I'm treated fairly here."

Jeremy sneered. "I suppose that means you want more money."

"No, but I would like leave to act as a reporter—the job for which I was hired—and not as a servant, on an ongoing basis. I'd like leave to develop further stories along this same view."

"You have more ideas? Like this?" Winton jumped on it.

"Plenty. I think the people of Boston need to know about their city and the individuals who live in it."

"Hmm. And you're sure O'Hare will grant you the rest of the interviews you've promised? He won't defect and run to one of the other papers?"

"He's given me his word, sir."

"Oh, and the word of an ignorant bog jumper is golden, is that it?"

Dorothea turned her eyes on Jeremy. "He's a skilled and articulate man. You must be mistaking lack of higher schooling with ignorance. All too plainly, the former does not prohibit the latter."

Jeremy leaned toward her across his father's desk. "Careful you don't get too big for your knickers. And careful, little girl, you don't fall for this hero you've created."

****

Curiously, few outside the newspaper office seemed to connect Dorothea with her byline. Even when she reached the rooming house, where they knew she worked for the *Guardian*, none of the girls tumbled to the fact that she might have written the article that had taken the city by storm.

Eight women lived beneath Mrs. Bennett's roof, all single and all employed in varying capacities. Most struggled to make ends meet; Dorothea's job at the *Guardian* paid her better than most. Two of the others worked in a laundry, one for a fishmonger, one as tea girl in a law office.

Mrs. Bennett had very strict rules about curfews and male callers. A girl who didn't reach home by nine o'clock would be locked out, and no excuses. Male callers weren't welcome under any circumstances.

"There'll be none of that here," she'd told Dorothea firmly when she first arrived. "I run a respectable house."

She ran a miserly house, Dorothea thought now as she returned from work just in time for supper. The house reeked of onions, and she wasn't surprised to see Mrs. Bennett's usual fare—a tureen of onion soup and two small loaves of bread that afforded her boarders one slice each, if they were quick enough.

She slid into her seat without hesitation. It had been a long, strange day that left her perished.

She interrupted a conversation already in progress as the bowls got filled and the bread passed.

"I've seen him, you know. During that demonstration last fall on the waterfront—the one where the fight broke out and so many workers got arrested. So many Irish." The speaker, Betsy, worked for the fishmonger. Like Dorothea, she must have come straight from her job; a faint pong of day-old fish came off her, competing rather nauseatingly with the smell of onions. She rolled her eyes, and her long face twisted into an expression of ecstasy. "He's ever so handsome."

"But he's Irish." This speaker, Margaret, glanced at Mrs. Bennett for approval. Mrs. Bennett would sooner starve than accept an Irish boarder.

"So? Some of those Irish blokes are ever so well set up and handsome."

"But dumb as stumps," contributed another girl. "Funny, the article didn't make him sound dumb."

Dorothea bit her lip and scooped a spoonful of unappetizing soup.

"He's battling for what he believes in," said another girl dreamily, "Irish or not."

"And," said Deborah, from the law office, "is it fair for a man to do the same work as another and get paid less?"

"But the Irish are thick on the ground. Most of them don't keep a job long anyway—they're drunk half the time. Why pay to keep 'em when you can just hire another one?"

"Still, if they have children to feed…"

"They wouldn't have so many children if they weren't all Catholics. I mean, its barely decent."

"And they treat their women badly—even if they are good-looking."

"Dorothea?" Someone finally focused on her. "You work at the *Guardian*, don't you? Do you know anything about the man who wrote the article?"

Did they not wonder why the journalist in question

had the same last name as she did? And they called O'Hare thick! To be fair, though, she'd forgotten most of their last names; no doubt they'd forgotten hers as well.

Before she could answer, Deborah asked, "Did O'Hare come to the office for his interview? Did you see him? Bring him tea?"

"No."

"I heard the interview was conducted at a secret location so no one from the *Herald* or the *Courier* could horn in."

"I just wondered if he's as handsome as Betsy says."

Yes, Dorothea thought. Oh, yes.

At that moment they all heard a knock at the house door. Mrs. Bennett hurried off and came back with a folded slip of paper which she immediately thrust in Dorothea's direction.

"For you."

Dorothea unfolded the paper while heat mounted in her face. On it was drawn a picture of a tea cup, complete with steam, and the words, *Tomorrow at four. Go around back.* in a bold, black hand she recognized.

She looked up to find everyone in the room staring at her and tucked the paper into her bosom. She'd begun a collection.

"That," Mrs. Bennett said, "had better not be from a man."

Chapter Ten

"They all think I'm a male reporter. For the time being, I'm going to remain on the low-down. But later—ah, later I'll set them straight."

Dorothea shared the news as she poured tea for both of them, once more in the back room at Sybil's. She felt much less nervous in O'Hare's company this time. In fact, she'd looked forward all day to meeting him, and her spirits ran high.

As always when happy, she chattered. She realized belatedly she'd barely stopped talking since she came in, through the back this time as requested.

Hare said little. He merely sat at his ease, watching her.

Smiling.

And oh, how handsome he looked—even more so than she remembered, and she'd remembered him well.

She halted her flow of chatter abruptly. "I'm so sorry. I haven't allowed you a word. My ma always says I'm like a runaway train when I get talking."

His smile deepened. What did she see in his eyes? Surely not admiration?

"You're a rare one, Dora Sinclair, and no mistake."

She pushed his tea cup across the table and pulled out her notebook. "So are you ready to do the next interview?"

"No."

"Mr. Winton plans to run one a week, but we can do the actual interviews anytime…" Her mind belatedly caught up with her tongue, and her heart sank. "No? Don't say you've changed your mind."

"I have not. And we can do the interviews any time you like. Today, though, I just wanted to thank you."

"Thank me?"

"It's a lovely piece of writing, Dora. Mostly fiction, though."

"I don't think so. I may have massaged the words a bit—embellished the sentiments—but it's all true, if you look at it. Everything you told me."

"I doubt the good people of this city have ever before given a thought to an Irish wean working ten hours on an empty stomach."

"That's the whole point, isn't it? To unite everyone in Boston beneath a single umbrella—that of being human."

"A fine sentiment, that, and your article was very persuasive. But I fear the soft feelings stop at the pocketbook."

"Maybe. Maybe not. Really, Hare, we're fighting for the same things—just in different ways."

"Fighting, are you?"

"Oh, yes, don't doubt it. I've never been able to tolerate injustice." She thought of her friend Jo, back home—a freed slave. "It trips something in me. I become furious. In this case, I'll fight with words."

"Mightier than the sword, eh?"

"They can be. And in conjunction with the sword—oh, just imagine!"

His gaze moved over her face. "I am. So I'm to man the bulwarks of the struggle, am I, while you work your magic behind the scenes?"

"Something like that."

"We're a team?"

Her gaze engaged and held his. "I hope so." She cleared her throat and asked, "What reaction have you had to the article?"

"I'm flaming famous among my friends and cohorts. Of course, everyone in the city knew my identity—half of them thought me a bully, the other half a mouthpiece. No one thought much about the reasons I'm fighting or that there are hundreds in this city just like me. Not till now."

"That's good, right?"

"It's good. People have been coming by the cabinet shop just to take a gander at me and stopping me on the street to shake my hand. The lady of the house where we're installing the new kitchen treated me to a half-hour diatribe about necessity. Apparently when she bargained down a price, she never thought about the bread she snatched from the mouths of hungry bairns."

"Till now."

"Till now."

"Then we've already accomplished something." Dorothea slid the plate of pastries closer. "I almost feel guilty having these when others haven't."

"Don't. I like seeing you enjoy them."

"Do you?"

"Yes."

Again their gazes touched and held. This time it felt like a physical embrace. Dorothea had a sudden, blinding image of what else she might enjoy with this man. Sweet mercy, what was the matter with her? She never entertained such thoughts.

She selected a pastry and pushed the plate at him. "You too."

"Nah, I'm fine with the tea." His gaze didn't flicker from hers. Why did she feel he implied he'd rather feast his eyes on her?

"You have an incredible face, Dora Sinclair. Do you know that? Lovely as a rose, and it shows everything you think."

Dorothea devoutly hoped not.

"So," she said quickly, "what do you think we should highlight with the next piece? I was thinking I'd focus on all the men who get dismissed out of hand, describe the reasons they're fighting, and outline what happens to their families as a consequence."

"Continuing the hungry child theme, eh?"

"More or less."

His graceful, brown fingers toyed with the plate. "How did you come up with that title, then? A Hungry Heart?"

"It just came to me. Things frequently do. I mean to expand upon it, show throughout the series that a heart can be hungry for more than food—for justice, respect, equality…"

"Love?"

"Love, certainly." Dorothea drew a breath.

"The men you're talking about, the ones who work sixteen-hour days for a pittance, who scrape their fingers bloody and break their backs only to be dismissed out of hand, who accept the insults, the slurs, and the injustice—that's why they do it. For love. Love of their wives and their bairns—the children society says they have by accident and don't value. This I've seen for truth."

"Then that's what I'll have to show through our interviews."

"There's a passion in the struggle for equality, Miss Dora—a quiet passion that beats in men's hearts. They spend themselves for those they love."

Breathless, Dorothea asked, "Is that what you do?"

"Me?" He shrugged. "I do it for love of them—for the sake of their valiant spirits. I've no one close to me now."

"No wife? No sweetheart?"

"Sweetheart, is it?" He grinned. "There are women. There are always women. They come and go like the tides. Not one has stayed."

Dorothea found that hard to believe. "Perhaps it's because you don't welcome them."

"Perhaps so." Laughter brimmed in his eyes. "Never say you mean to write a story about my romantic exploits."

"People might be interested. The girls at Mrs. Bennett's would."

"I doubt that. By any road, it's scarcely relevant." He wagged his eyebrows at her. "Enjoy that Napoleon, did you?"

"Very much." Unthinking, Dorothea licked her fingers; O'Hare's eyes narrowed.

"You missed a bit there."

"I beg your pardon?"

"Cream at the corner of your mouth." Languidly, he reached across the table and used his finger to scoop away the errant blob of filling. Dorothea froze where she sat, while sensation spiked through her and her heart took up a slow, throbbing rhythm.

"Can't have you looking anything but the proper

lady now, can we?"

"No." Dorothea tore her eyes from his and focused them on her notebook. "So…so our next effort will showcase the men involved in the struggle, as you call it, and their families. Only these are meant to be interviews with you, so it will all have to come through your m-mouth. Mr. Winton was very specific about that. Otherwise I feel I have fairly free license, which is quite extraordinary in the newspaper business. I can't even tell you. No reporter gets that kind of leeway, least to say one who's a virtual unknown—"

"Dora."

"Reporters have to work years and years for this kind of opportunity, so you see I'm really the one who should be thanking you—"

"Dora!"

"Yes?"

"Breathe, lass."

"Eh?"

"You're running on something fierce."

"Oh, yes, I guess I am. Will—"

He reached across the table again and covered her hand with his. The sheer heat of his touch silenced her.

I can't do this, I can't be around him. Not when he affects me this way. Why does he affect me this way?

"I did warn you," she addressed their joined hands.

"Warn me of what?"

"That I tend to talk too much when I'm—excited." Heat stained her cheeks at the implication. He withdrew his hand and laughed softly.

That made her glare. "Are you scoffing at me?"

"No. Never." He laid his hand on his heart. "I wouldn't dare. You're much too earnest. Anyway, there's nothing to scoff at. You're right; this is a sterling opportunity for both of us."

Still addressing her notebook she said, "I think we should approach this through the medium of employment. Talk about your job at the cabinetmaker's, how you got it and all, then veer into the lack of opportunities for other Irish, no matter how skilled or unskilled."

"That's an intelligent plan."

"Then you approve?"

"I do. With one addition."

She lifted her eyes to his. "What's that?"

"I think, before you write the piece, you should meet one of these families."

Enthusiasm flooded her. "Oh, yes. You just give me their direction and—"

"No, it doesn't work like that. They won't talk to you, won't even let you in, unless I introduce you."

"Very well. Can you think of a particular family?"

"There are dozens. But Terry Gallagher's comes to mind."

"How many children?"

"Six, and Deirdre's expecting."

"We'll take them some pastries. I'll bet they've never tasted the like. Might we?"

Again he studied her before he said, "All right. I'll pick some up on the way. Tomorrow night?"

"Fine, but we'd better meet here. It wouldn't do for you to come to the rooming house."

He winked at her. "Five o'clock?"

Dorothea couldn't wait.

Chapter Eleven

O'Hare stole yet another look at the woman beside him. For the sake of her continued anonymity he'd hired a cab—not that anyone would tumble to her identity as D. R. Sinclair if they saw her with him. Female reporters were far too rare. More likely folks would consider her his fancy piece.

But she didn't look that part, either. As he'd said yesterday, she was too much the lady. Today she wore the blue hat he'd rescued for her on the waterfront—somewhat repaired—and a fetching little outfit with a short jacket and blue piping all round.

She'd spent every minute since they'd met telling him about refurbishing the hat, brushing away the dried grit and mending the veil with tiny stitches she hoped wouldn't show. She went on and on about her ma being a seamstress, as well as her best friend—the one married to her apprenticed blacksmith not-quite-brother—and how, despite all that, skill with a needle never came easily to her.

She could talk—sweet Jesus, how the woman could talk! The fact that she didn't give him a chance to insert a word meant she felt either happy or nervous.

O'Hare didn't mind. He liked listening to her, letting the conversation sort of wash over him like water onto a shore. He liked being alone with her in the cab, as well, just the two of them together—enjoyed the way it made him feel and how he could catch the delicate scent of her, mingled roses and woman.

He even liked the way she clutched the white bakery box from Sybil's, balancing it against every bump and turn to protect the contents. How could he explain to her that Terry's bairns wouldn't care if she brought a sack of crumbs—it had been so long since they had a treat.

Still, it was a kind gesture on her part, and something he wouldn't have considered. He spent his time thinking about fundamentals like keeping the Gallaghers' rent paid. A treat, as he knew, could be just as important.

He'd never celebrated a birthday when young. In fact, when he was eight, he'd had to ask his ma when his birthday was; all his friends knew theirs—he didn't.

"It's in May," she'd told him and taken a vague stab at it. "The twenty-first?"

He focused hastily on what Dora was saying just as she paused for breath. "Words. For me it's always been about words."

He wondered what she'd do if he kissed her right here in the gloom of the stuffy cab. He bet she'd stop talking then. Maybe even drop the box of pastries.

That would be a damn shame.

"What?" she inquired, peering at him. "Why are you smiling?"

"Am I smiling?"

"Yes."

"Must be your matchless company. Hold on now, lass; we've arrived."

The Gallaghers shared three cramped rooms at the top of an ugly house in a narrow street, and glad to have them. Since Terry had been thrown out of work last winter, they'd paid the rent in a variety of ways, including through collections raised by their friends. O'Hare knew Terry Gallagher for a proud man who rarely took a drink and wanted only to work—at variance with the caricature of the Irishman rife in this city.

He wondered what Dora, with her compassionate heart, would make of the family.

Deirdre Gallagher, leading with her great belly, opened the door to his knock and greeted them with a dignified nod. A bonny woman was Deirdre, with pretty blue eyes and glossy brown hair now twisted into the semblance of a bun.

"Will you not come in?"

Terry stepped up then, a big shuffling man who shook O'Hare's hand and gave Dorothea an uncertain look. Terry had needed to be talked into this. He didn't relish having his personal business splashed all over the city, he'd declared, but at last he'd been persuaded by the prospect of helping other families like his.

The children stood in a silent row, the eldest, Graine, with the youngest, Matty, in her arms. Pity tugged at O'Hare's heart when he saw how Deirdre had done her best to clothe them all for the occasion in garments passed down so many times they were faded to gray. He remembered the winter he'd had nothing for his feet but a broken, ill-fitting pair of shoes found in the trash, shoes he'd had to tie to his feet.

He felt for these bairns.

"Oh, what a beautiful family! Here—we brought these." Dorothea thrust the white box of pastries at Deirdre. "I hope you'll share them around."

It took precisely five minutes for Dorothea's warmth to thaw Deirdre Gallagher, ten for Terry to lose his stiff pride and lean toward her confidingly at the kitchen table. The children loved her from the moment their ma opened the white box.

And after all, O'Hare had to say little. He just sat, drank the weak tea Deirdre gave him, and watched while Dorothea Sinclair worked her magic.

It lay in her words, her impulsive sympathy, and the thoughtless respect she offered her hosts. It shone through the kindness in her lovely eyes which, more than once, filled with tears.

She scribbled lines and lines of notes, all while continuing to listen with the utmost attention. In the end, Terry Gallagher tapped her notebook and asked, "You think it will help, this story o' yours?"

"I believe it will, Mr. Gallagher, I sincerely do. Otherwise I wouldn't be doing this."

"You just make sure you put in there that I want to work, mind. I'd work twenty-four hours a day if I had to, to keep my family from want. All I'm asking is a fair chance."

"I'll do my best to make my readers understand that, Mr. Gallagher."

"And feel it, miss." Deirdre scrubbed tears from her cheeks. "If only they could feel what I feel, putting my weans to bed at night, knowing they've not had enough to eat. And this new one coming—I fear for him, so I do."

Dorothea Sinclair might have nodded, she might have made promises and added to her notes. Instead, she reached across the table and gave Deirdre Gallagher a hug. The two women embraced like old friends—or rather, O'Hare thought, like new ones.

"I wish there were more I could do to help your family."

"'Tis not just us," Terry told her earnestly. "There are dozens like us throughout Boston, men who get dismissed when they raise the slightest request, who get tossed out and have to go home and tell their families…" His voice broke.

Deirdre took it up. "And they call us lazy! My husband is not lazy, miss! I've seen him work like a draft horse at jobs no one else would touch, for pennies. Pennies!"

"I understand." Dorothea gripped her notebook. "And I will do my best. But you make me feel humbled, putting so much faith in me."

O'Hare's heart stirred in his chest. He did not want to entertain feelings for Dorothea Sinclair. She represented temptation enough already, with her rosy cheeks and glorious, midnight-dark hair. This thing they undertook together was much too important for him to muck it up with his *feelings*.

"Are we finished, Miss Sinclair?" he asked softly.

"I think so, yes." She got to her feet and offered Terry and Deirdre her hand in turn. "It's been an honor meeting you, and speaking with you." She smiled at Deirdre. "Good luck with the baby. When are you due?"

Deirdre's face lit. "Within the month."

"I have a new baby brother back home in Maine. His name's Andy."

"Ah, and isn't that just the name we plan on if this one's a boy?" Deirdre clasped Dorothea's hand in both of hers. "Bless you, miss."

85

O'Hare laid his finger aside his nose. "And not a word, now, that D. R. Sinclair is a *miss*. We're keeping that under our hats for the time. It'll get out eventually, just not yet."

O'Hare steadied Dorothea's elbow going down the steep, narrow stairs, wondering again why he felt so stirred by this woman at his side. Sweet and genuine, smart and beautiful—how then could he fail to be stirred?

He saw her into the cab and climbed in after her. A few minutes alone before he had to part with her again.

"You're unusually silent, Miss Dora."

She looked at him in the soft gloom. "I'm wondering if I can do their story justice. So much rides on it."

"You can."

"I'm not sure—"

"Dora, lass, you *can*."

Her gaze clung to his. "How can you be certain?"

"Because you were marvelous back there. You have a rare ability to affect people. Don't underestimate it."

"I wish—I wish I could find Terry Gallagher a job, a good one. I wish I could take the worry from his wife's eyes. I wish those children could have cakes every day and never, *never* go to bed hungry."

She swiped her cheeks, much as Deirdre had.

"Don't weep, lass."

"I can't help it. Did you see their faces when they tasted those pastries? Did you?"

"Yes."

"And can you imagine going without?"

He could; he had. It made a wide gulf between

them, because she couldn't imagine what he'd lived, so well had her blacksmith father and her seamstress mother taken care of her.

Yet she had a heart capable of making a leap across that distance. And there in the cab he wanted nothing so much as to take her in his arms and kiss her, make an intimate acquaintance with all the warmth that lay in store for the man—the one lucky man—upon whom she might bestow it.

Not him. Surely not him. They were crusaders together, nothing more.

And surely he'd long ago outgrown wanting things he couldn't have.

Chapter Twelve

Dorothea paused at the door of Sybil's shop to shake the wet from her coat before going in. Blustery rain held Boston in its grip, and night had fallen with preternatural speed. Barely five o'clock and it looked like midnight, the streets shining where the lamplight hit them.

The weather reminded Dorothea of home, where storms tended to blow across Frenchman Bay to strike the little house that faced the ocean so bravely, the one where she'd grown up.

A sharp pang of homesickness gripped her. She'd received not one but two letters from home today, the first from her mother and the other from Jo Grier, and she ached to be there with them, drinking tea and talking the way they used to.

That couldn't happen, not right now. Besides, a third missive had been delivered to the *Guardian* office—a folded paper bearing nothing but a drawing of a hare, a tea cup, and the numeral five.

She knew what that meant by now. She should—she saw it often enough.

Two weeks had passed, and Sybil's had become her and O'Hare's accepted meeting place. It had also become her port in a storm of some magnitude—the series about Hare O'Hare progressed wonderfully. Montgomery Winton had decided to run her stories twice a week, on Tuesdays and Thursdays, and couldn't be more pleased with how the papers continued to sell.

Everyone in the city read the stories Dorothea penned. The Wintons—father and son—might not appreciate the content; they might denounce it as soft, slanted, even sensationalized. But Montgomery Winton printed the stories anyway, word for word just as Dorothea penned them, because the people of Boston, of all classes, simply couldn't get enough. They read for various reasons, some to feed a hunger, some to denounce her and the struggle upon which she shone a light. But they read, and on the two days a week her stories ran, circulation more than tripled.

And Dorothea teetered on the edge of being discovered. Everyone in Boston speculated over the identity of D. R. Sinclair. Forays had been made into the *Guardian* office, where most everyone now guessed. A number of people in O'Hare's world knew the truth, as well.

It wouldn't remain secret much longer.

She walked into the warmth of the shop and came face to face with Sybil. The woman frequently seemed to materialize from thin air, and this afternoon, with the gloom gathering outside and the candles on the tables flickering, she presented an aspect that raised all Dorothea's ancestral superstitions.

"Oh, Sybil, you startled me."

Sybil narrowed her eyes and leaned close. A wave of patchouli assaulted Dorothea's senses.

"You," Sybil said.

"I beg your pardon?"

"I dreamed of you last night."

Oh! thought Dorothea, and what does one say to

such a pronouncement?

Sybil gave her no time to decide. "A dream it was from the Other World. You are to be the one."

"I'm sorry, I don't understand. Is our mutual friend here? He sent for me."

"And so you come, you run to him. Are you ready to give your heart?"

Funny she should ask that. Jo's letter had hinted at something similar. Jo often had presentiments about things, and out of the blue she'd asked if Dorothea had been seeing anyone.

If so, she wrote, *better hang onto him.*

"You must let me do a reading for you," Sybil whispered spectrally. "The leaves. Or better yet, the cards."

Dorothea experienced what her father, from Scotland, called the *cauld grue*. Straight from the Highlands, he'd told her stories of the seers there and how no one dared doubt their veracity.

"Perhaps another time."

"Soon." Sybil nodded. "Soon." She gestured to the door at the back of the near-empty tearoom. "Go in."

Dorothea did, with alacrity. Usually when she let herself into the back parlor she found Hare lounging at the table behind his cup of tea, tawny eyes half hooded. Now she caught him on his feet and pacing, his face alight with excitement.

"Dora," he greeted her. "Glorious lass!"

"What is it? What's happened?" He made her breathless when she saw him like this, burning like copper flame. She hurried to the table and set down her bag.

He treated her to a smile that rendered her weak in

the knees, came around the table, and swept her up in his arms.

Oh, and it felt sublime! How many times while together had she longed to feel his arms around her? How often had she wanted, while they sat talking, to lean across the table and press her lips to his cheek, brush against the copper stubble that sprouted there—or better yet, against his lips? Not wise, she knew, to cross that line. Besides, she wasn't that kind of girl. Was she?

Now he took the choice to resist out of her hands, pulled her hard against him and swung her around, feet off the floor.

Her hat fell off, and she went dizzy—not from the motion.

She gazed into his face. "Hare?"

He returned her glance, the golden eyes almost too bright at close quarters, his warmth a tangible force. His gaze devoured her face, caressing every feature before he said, "Do you know what you've done?"

"I don't."

"Only worked a miracle with that clever pen of yours." He caught her fingers in his, raised them to his lips, and kissed them. Heat blossomed throughout Dorothea, kicking her in the belly like a draft horse.

"What—!"

"Terry Gallagher has a job. Someone who read your story—a man with a delivery business—went out of his way to locate him and offer him the place. And it's a good place, too, not some piecemeal job on the docks where he'll get dismissed at a whim, but one with security. And the best part?" He squeezed her tighter. "The man—his employer—is non-Irish. That means, my girl, you're reaching the hearts and minds of everyone in this city. So you see, it's all down to you."

"Oh, my!" Dorothea squeaked out. "That's just the very best news!"

"Terry came to tell me. Beside himself with happiness he was. He said Deirdre wept when she heard."

Tears flooded Dorothea's eyes also. "So we're making a difference?"

"You can bet we are. Here now. I didn't mean to make you cry." He set her down and gently thumbed a tear from her cheek. Still within the circle of his arms, Dorothea froze, caught by his gaze which changed abruptly from euphoria to something so intense it pulled at her soul.

"Beautiful lass," he murmured, and she felt the warm brush of his lips on her other cheek, kissing rather than brushing the tears away. She stirred then, sliding her hands up his chest and around his neck as she leaned into him. Effortlessly, instinctively, they moved together so their lips met in a first soft, fleeting contact before clinging tight.

Desire flared and sensation tore through her, blossoming up from a place deep inside. He tasted warm and wild and sweet; he felt like a part of her long missing. This felt like coming home.

His lips wooed hers, persuaded them apart and sought admittance to all she was. She parted for him so she might taste more, and he poured into her, first his tongue stroking her tongue and the insides of her lips and cheeks in caress after caress, then his essence. She felt his strength, his compassion, and the hunger burgeoning from his heart.

Her knees went weak, and she hung onto him,

knowing she never, never wanted to let go.

But he broke the kiss with a lingering contact of lips on lips and set her from him gently. Instead of moving away from her, he touched his forehead to hers; the thick, copper lashes swept down to cover his eyes.

"I'll not apologize for that, though I suppose I should. I've wanted to kiss you since the first time I saw you on the waterfront."

"Yes." Dorothea, filled with the delightful flavor of him, strong like Irish whiskey, licked her lips. "But—but probably not a line we should cross."

"Crossed now." Still he didn't release her; instead his arms tightened. "What to do about it?"

What, indeed? Dorothea knew what she wanted to do, and it shocked her. Gently bred women of good family didn't throw themselves at men, even men who triggered desire and oozed charm to this extent.

Yet all she could imagine right now was kissing him again, setting her hands roving down from his shoulders inside his shirt, fusing with the wonderful warmth he exuded, giving herself to him.

Unwise. Very unwise.

She gazed into his face earnestly. "What do you want to do?"

His lashes swept back up. "Only you would ask me such a question, Dora Sinclair. Honest to the bone, you are."

"There's no sense being any other way."

"True. And in all honesty, it would be madness for us to become involved…romantically."

Dorothea's heart plummeted. But she said, "I suppose you're right." Then why didn't he leave go of her?

"I value you as a friend. I value what we're accomplishing together for the likes of Terry Gallagher."

"As do I."

"I wouldn't want to muck that up. And romantic involvements—well, they frequently end badly."

"Do they?"

"All too often. And one thing I know, Dorothea Sinclair—I'm not good enough for the likes of you."

She stiffened in indignation on his behalf. "Why do you say that?"

His gaze caressed her face. "Just look at you: clever and brim full of talent, as well as beautiful—so beautiful. You deserve a man who can fulfill your dreams, treat you as you've a right to expect."

"And who might that be?" she returned, her heart in her eyes.

"A man of learning, of some means—one who can provide you a fine home and a life of comfort. Children—" He faltered over that last word, and his eyes heated. "I am none of those things, lass."

"Shouldn't I have leave to decide what I deserve?"

"No. You're too likely to choose with your heart and not your head. You don't know me—"

"I don't?" Her brows flew up. "Sir, am I not your personal biographer? I know more about you than anyone in this city. After four articles together…"

"And two to go."

"And two to go, how can you say I don't know you? Hare O'Hare, I've looked into your heart."

"That's just it, though, Dora. It's not even my real name. You know of me only what I've told you."

"And what I've felt. You mention my dreams…"

She'd had dreams, yes: marriage some day at an indistinct time in the future to a shadowy figure, perhaps a professor-type gentleman with whom she might share the joys of reading and conversation. Eventually she wanted a family too, lively as the one back home. In her mind—deep down—warmth and family were synonymous with home.

None of that fit this man. And as she now saw, her vision of a husband had allowed little enough for love. What if the love came first, swept her off her feet, made her throw caution to the winds?

What if life sent her something she'd never imagined, this hunger uniting two hearts?

"My dreams," she told Hare slowly and decidedly, "are things that come to me in the night. This—you—are reality."

"Now, lass…"

"Best not to try and tell me what to do—or how to feel. It just makes me stubborn. That's one of my faults. You've already made acquaintance with some of the others—such as talking too much. But I've sterling qualities as well, like my determination. And my loyalty. Once I decide on something—someone—I'm true to the end."

"I don't doubt it. But please, *please*, lass, don't decide on me."

How could she tell him it was already too late? Her heart had chosen, and her desire followed. He might be the last person on earth she should be with. That would change nothing.

He sighed, and she felt it pass through him.

"Don't do this, Dora. Please don't break your heart over me."

She stepped away from him. "We shall see, shan't we? Meanwhile, we've two more articles to write."

Chapter Thirteen

"There is a woman, isn't there?" Marielle paused in the act of walking past Hare into the tea room and fixed him with a discerning look from bright blue eyes.

He lifted his eyebrows. "Now, why would you say that?"

She smiled, a confident curl of the lips. "Just look at you—I can see it plain, lad. You might as well write it all over your face."

O'Hare cursed silently. Women, with their knowing and their choosing. Exasperating creatures, they were.

"I don't wish to talk about it." He scarcely dared think about Dora Sinclair for the way it made him feel. To be sure, there'd been women in the past—plenty of women. He trifled with them when lonely and quite frankly used them when in need. But none who twisted up his heart inside, made him feel at once protective and helpless.

He didn't like feeling helpless; he'd long ago sworn to put that emotion behind him. If he had to jettison love also, then so be it.

Marielle swept into the rear parlor where he and Dora had met so often—the very place O'Hare had kissed her. Held her in his arms. Tasted the fire and innocence that combined impossibly to make a potent temptation.

"Who is she? And how far has it gone?"

O'Hare's annoyance with Marielle—or was it with himself?—increased a notch. He should be able to put Dorothea Sinclair out of his mind. It had just been a kiss.

One single kiss.

And now he wanted more, wanted to experience again the heady delight of merging his lips with hers and tasting the delectable mix of girl and woman. He wanted to stoke that fire inside her, see how hot he could make it burn.

"Lad?" He realized Marielle had spoken several times. "Shut the door. We have business."

Sybil's had just closed, Marielle waiting till the patrons had gone. She would need to get home safely and soon.

He shut the door and joined her at the table. No selection of pastries tonight. Marielle had no need for him to provide her with delicacies or to kiss her senseless.

That kiss. He remembered the look on Dora's face after—the look in her beautiful, dreamy eyes—as if someone had simultaneously slapped her and given her a gift that took her breath away.

He wouldn't need to breathe if he were with her. Neither of them would. He'd wrap her in his arms and…

"You're miles away." Marielle interrupted him once again. "Perhaps this will focus your attention."

She drew an envelope from her bag and tossed it on the table. A wad of bills slid halfway out.

"What's this?"

"You asked for money, didn't you? A contribution

to the cause. That article your reporter friend wrote got to me. Got to Mr. Dickenson, in fact. He made a gift of that."

Stunned, O'Hare sat down at the table. "So much?"

"I added some of my own funds. As I say, what are a few ribbons or new slippers when my people are in need?"

"Bless you, Marielle."

She eyed him again. "The least I can do—the very least. You've turned into quite the hero, haven't you? It was clever, agreeing to these interviews. They've made you…human."

"I hope so. Of course, it's not my clever writing that's worked the magic."

"No. That of Mr. D. R. Sinclair. Mr. Dickenson says rumor runs rife as to his identity and that employees at the *Guardian* have been sworn to silence at penalty of losing their jobs. But you know the truth of it."

"I do."

She leaned across the table impulsively. "So tell me."

"It needs to be kept secret for now."

He shuddered at the thought of Dorothea in the hands of anti-Irish hardliners. Some of those bastards had absolutely no scruples and couldn't be happy with what her series had prompted.

"You can trust me. I'll not breathe a word, not even to Mr. Dickenson."

"Not that I don't trust you, Marielle—I do. But it's not my safety at stake." He raked her with a glance. "And tell me, do you call the man Mr. Dickenson even in bed?"

To his surprise her cheeks grew pink, the first crack he'd seen in her composure for quite some time.

"Never mind me, lad. But as a matter of fact, I have some news on that front—just for your ears, now, at least for the time being. Come next winter, given all goes well, I'll be presenting Mr. Dickenson with a child—a son, if the angels smile on me."

"Will you, then?" O'Hare eyed her with some amazement. Exquisitely clad as always, blonde hair shining and waist trim… "Now, there's a surprise. When you married him, you swore it would never happen."

"Yes, well, just so you know, he's uncommonly pleased with me at present." She nodded at the envelope. "Which means I should be able to get more of that. How dire is the need, lad?"

"Dire. You're not the only one breeding in Boston. A lot of bairns will be born to want."

"Not mine," she said in satisfaction. "He'll land square in the lap of luxury. That doesn't mean I don't care about the others. When that lot runs out, send me a message, right?"

"I will. And thank you, sweetheart."

"Now." Marielle leaned toward him again. "I've told you my deepest, darkest secret. You have to tell me yours."

"I don't, minx."

"Who is she?"

"There's no *she*."

Marielle's blue eyes gleamed as she sat back and folded her hands. "Well, now. Like most men, you're a decent liar—maybe even better than most. But you don't fool me. I can fair smell her on you."

"Don't be daft."

"Hmm, let's see. The daughter of one of your cronies? No, I think not. A maid in one of the great houses? Ah, now there's a possible tableau: you found her crying over her mistreatment, and that soft heart you hide so well got the better of you... But no, you must have met dozens of such during your time. Not one has ever turned your head before. Surely not a doxy. Though it could happen, if your heart tripped you up, I guess. And I know for a fact they're the only women you usually see."

"You've always bragged on your woman's intuition, Marielle. If it's all you claim, you should need me to tell you naught."

The blue eyes narrowed, as Marielle considered him, before widening with sudden comprehension. She snapped her fingers.

"The reporter—D. R. whatever it is. Never say it's a woman?"

O'Hare gaped at her in consternation, and she laughed.

"Well, well, my lad—I can see the attraction, then. All that warmth and compassion—and the intelligence—wrapped up in one package. You've always had a weakness for intelligence. Is she pretty, too?"

"Not a word of this, Marielle."

"It will get out eventually."

"Yes, it will. But so far no one's broken the story. And I wouldn't want to endanger her in any way when she's doing such stellar work for us."

"And when you fancy her so."

"I didn't say that."

"You don't have to. I always knew when you finally fell, you'd fall hard."

"It's not like that."

"What's it like, then?"

O'Hare thought about Dorothea Sinclair. Desire all wrapped up in an adorable, funny, impulsive package. He shook his head.

"Ah," Marielle crooned, "he has no words—the man with the honeyed tongue cannot even describe his goddess. Are you going to marry her?"

He stared. "Are you mad?"

"I don't think so."

"Marielle, she's not for the likes of me."

"Why not?"

"She's educated, respectable—"

"You're respectable enough."

"You know where I came from. What I came from."

"As did half the folks in this city. Love's a rare thing, boyo. And if she's all that respectable, I'd guess marriage is your only choice."

O'Hare widened his eyes at her. "You're wrong. Keeping shut about my feelings is the only choice."

****

Dorothea's steps slowed when she reached the *Guardian*'s offices next morning. Watery sunlight flowed over the building and illuminated the throng gathered in front of the steps. Had there been an accident? She hoped not, but at this hour delivery trucks sometimes collided. Once she'd seen a newsboy run down almost at the door.

Right now all she could see were the backs of the onlookers, mostly men in suits, no doubt on their way to jobs in the business district.

She didn't need the delay this morning. In her bag she had her fifth story, which she'd sat up writing most of the night and which had prompted a flood of ideas for other stories to follow the original series. She wanted to speak with Mr. Winton about that, pin him down while she still had some leverage.

She pushed her way through the crowd, using her elbows to good advantage. The men in the group started indignantly until they noticed her gender; then for the most part they moved aside courteously, and she gained the front of the throng, where she saw an incredible sight.

A man stood on a wooden crate about thirty feet from the *Guardian*'s entrance, pontificating. He wore the garb of a gentleman—dark gray morning coat, white shirt, and flowing cravat—and had the voice of an actor aiming at the back rows of the theater. Her quick eye for detail noted he needed a proper haircut and his shoes wanted shining.

Not a genuine gentleman, then.

She paused, her ears nearly curling at what they heard.

"…is a monster seeking the overthrow of good and honorable people in this town. Will we bow before him and his ilk? No! We have been fighters since the first. Did we quail when we tossed tea into that harbor? Did we falter when the British invaded? No! Will we be overrun now by Irish rabble with delusions about their station?"

Dorothea stiffened where she stood.

"Filthy, uneducated, breeding like rats—these folks will overtake us if we allow it. This man, as I say, is no hero!" He waved what Dorothea belatedly recognized for an issue of the *Guardian*, her first byline, with a caricature of O'Hare pinned beneath it.

All the blood drained from her face and flooded back in a rush. She squeezed her hands into fists.

"The Irish in this city should be grateful to us. We employ them in our businesses, in our houses. We put food in the mouths of their ever-increasing broods. But are they satisfied? No. Do you know, ladies and gentlemen, how many Irish now reside here in Boston? Why, were they to rise up as one, they might well overthrow the honest, hardworking people of our town."

And, thought Dorothea furiously, would he have them believe there were no hardworking Irish in Boston? Did those lasses in the big houses not work twenty hours a day for little more than their keep? Did men like Terry Gallagher not take on any filthy job they could?

Were O'Hare's graceful hands not scarred from labor? And why had they made *him* their poster boy for hate and the lies this man spewed—pinned *his* likeness up there as a target for all to see?

The truth hit her with the force of a hurricane. Because of her. All for her vanity and her desire for a byline.

That realization turned her stomach sour and had her heart pounding up in her ears, making it difficult to hear when the poisonous diatribe went on. But she could feel the emotions of those around her as they caught the ugliness from the speaker like a contagion.

One sentence only penetrated the roar in Dorothea's head.

"Men like Hare O'Hare cannot be tolerated. They must be hunted down like diseased rats and destroyed."

Chapter Fourteen

"Someone here to see you." Ron Murray stuck his head into the back room, where O'Hare worked fitting the trim on a cabinet.

O'Hare paused and looked up. "Oh?"

And just like that, Dorothea Sinclair bustled in. Funny, because he'd been busy thinking of her and his superstitious side made him wonder if those thoughts conjured her now. For she couldn't be here, shouldn't be here.

But maybe it wasn't all that strange, he thought as he slowly straightened. Lately he'd been doing nothing but thinking of her and reliving that damn kiss.

Funny how she became prettier every time he saw her, even though she came in now looking worried, the dark hair mussed beneath her little hat, cheeks blooming. What did he see in her eyes?

"Something's wrong," he said, all too aware that Ron lingered and listened. "What is it?"

"We have a problem. I just came from—"

"Whisht. How did you find me?"

"You said the name of the place you're employed during one of our meetings. I am a reporter, after all."

O'Hare glared at Ron, who blinked in comprehension. "You'll want your privacy, I s'pose." He backed out and shut the door.

Dorothea came closer, and O'Hare sensed her

emotions still more clearly: distressed and jittery as a spooked pony.

"People are cognizant of where Hare O'Hare works, you know. Even though I didn't put it in the article, it isn't exactly a secret. Anybody could come here, walk right in. Attack you."

"I guess so, but…"

She sucked in a breath. "You're taking an awful chance with your safety, during this crusade of yours. I don't know why I never realized that at the start, but it's been brought home to me today."

"Why, what happened today?"

She began to pace in the limited space of the workroom, her skirts stirring up little clouds of sawdust as she moved.

"You wouldn't believe what I've seen—and heard. I'm on my lunch hour. I don't have much time, but I had to come and warn you. They want to stop you, are talking about hunting you down."

O'Hare stepped out from behind the half-assembled unit. Gently, he caught her shoulders between his hands and halted her steps. "Who is this?"

She stared into his face, her eyes bright with distress. "There was a protest in front of the *Guardian* office. A man was up on a box, spewing hate. He had an issue of the paper—our first article—and someone drew a caricature of you. A big crowd had gathered, Hare, and they were all with him. He preached nothing less than your destruction."

"It's all right."

"No, it isn't! It's a threat to your safety, to your life. He encouraged gangs of upright citizenry—that's what he called them, can you imagine?—to hunt you and other men like you down so the Irish can't gain the upper hand in Boston. You might be waylaid anywhere after dark. Beaten. Killed."

"Hush. Hush now, Dora. Did you suppose I didn't think of that?"

"What?"

"The danger's always been there. Men want to silence those who speak out. There are gangs of 'citizenry,' as you call them, and Anglo toffs also. There've been confrontations on the waterfront and many a broken head."

"But then—well, then you shouldn't have agreed to do the interviews. Because now all the attention's focused on you. That's what I've done. I've given them a target, and the way I see it, it's just a matter of time before something awful happens to you, and when it does, it will be all my fault!"

The sentence ended in a wail; tears now stood in her beautiful eyes, which no longer looked dreamy but frantic.

"Not your fault, Dora. No. Do you think me an idiot? I knew what would come of this. But it's a fight I had to take on. I'm a man, and I'm not about to run from the possibility of a confrontation or two."

"This isn't a confrontation or two. Don't you understand? They're bent on murder. And I couldn't bear it—simply couldn't bear it—if something happened to you."

She cast herself into his arms and knowledge struck through him like the deep tolling of a bell. When had this connection formed between them? When he returned her hat to her? The first time they sat together, talking? When he confided to her so much of himself, more than to anyone else ever? When they kissed?

Now she wept in his arms—wept for him, dammit—and pain pricked his heart like a cut from a knife. For this couldn't be. It couldn't be, it couldn't…

Before long, being Dora, she drew away, scrubbed the tears from her cheeks, and looked him in the eyes. "I think I'm falling in love with you."

"Ah, no, Dora—sweetheart, lovely darling—no."

"Don't tell me *no*."

"But it's impossible. A travesty. Not at all right for you."

"Not something I can help, you mean. It isn't as if I chose to have feelings for you. I'm surprised half the women in this city don't. And if you didn't want me to love you, you shouldn't be so—so…"

Despite himself, he cocked his head at her. "So—what?"

"I don't have words—dammit!"

"Dorothea Sinclair without words? I think hell must have just frozen over."

"Make jest of me if you will."

"I'm not. By God's truth, Dora, I am not." Should he tell her he had feelings for her too? That she now dwelt ceaselessly in his mind and whispered always to his heart? That he couldn't hear a funny story or see a child laugh without wanting to share it with her?

Or that he thought her the finest, most upright, beautiful, and intelligent woman he'd ever known?

No, no, no. Because she was all those things, and involvement with him could only harm her.

"Look, sweetheart, all this—what you think you feel for me—is likely the product of what we've shared, the passion of this fight we're staging together."

109

Light sparked in her eyes. "Don't tell me how I feel, Hare O'Hare. People have come to grief trying to tell me how I feel."

"Faith, I don't doubt it. But I'll not have you breaking your heart over me, Dora Sinclair. Before I see that happen, I'll walk away from it all, scuttle the rest of the stories…"

"And my career along with them?"

"Eh?"

"If I don't finish the series, I toss that away also."

"At the *Guardian*, maybe, but you're a brilliant writer. You could go anywhere else, tell them what you've written, who you are, and get taken on in a heartbeat."

She went very still; her gaze searched his. "You think I'm a brilliant writer?"

"I know you are."

"Oh!" She threw herself at him again, this time in a fit of ecstatic passion. Before he could react, her lips claimed his in a kiss of searing intensity and heat. By the time his stunned senses caught up, she had her arms twined around his neck, her body pressed tight to his, and her tongue seeking admittance to his mouth.

He let her in. Hell, he'd defy any man to resist. For she was all sweetness, that beguiling blend of child and woman and wise philosopher.

She might have been made to suit his heart.

But no—he couldn't allow such thoughts to overtake him, even though she answered his hunger on all levels. For a friend unswerving and true. For a woman eager for his bed. For a sorceress able to understand and answer the tangle of need and longing in his mind.

By the time he acknowledged all that, he'd given in and kissed her thoroughly, searching out every drop of her sweetness and drawing it into him until she went limp in his arms. When the kiss ended, she sighed deeply and laid her head against his shoulder.

Ah, and could she hear his heart pounding? Thumping like a drum, for need of her?

God help him.

"There, now," she murmured. "I feel complete."

"Dora—"

She picked up her head and looked at him, and the enchantress who wove magic so easily gazed out of her eyes. "Say what you will. Those wonderful lips of yours can form whatever words you like. Spurn me. Deny me… I'll not believe it. For I felt what I just felt. You care for me, too."

He loved her. Why try to deny it? She'd already said it out; he owed her the same honesty.

But survival instinct—on her behalf, not his— reared up. "Dora, I'm utterly and completely wrong for you."

"Oh, and do you think you're what I imagined for myself, Hare O'Hare?"

"No?"

"No. I thought if I ever found a man with whom I wanted to share my life, he'd be an intellectual, maybe a bit of a stuffed shirt, nice to look at but no Adonis. Certainly not brimming with charm and wit and enough male attractiveness to make me abandon my best intentions—"

O'Hare tried to feel insulted and failed, being far too intrigued. "And just what might this 'abandoning your best intentions' involve?"

"You don't want to know." She leaned close enough to brush his lips with hers. "Or maybe you do." She kissed him again, and his pulse leaped alarmingly. "You know," she whispered, "I'd slip away with you if you asked."

"Slip away?"

"To your room. We can't go to mine. Too many women there, and Mrs. Bennett would have apoplexy."

"Dorothea Sinclair!" Shocking. And utterly delightful. "You're a minx."

"Only around you. With everyone else I'm most straight-laced."

Yes, and he'd like to undo those laces…the last thing she needed. Trying to sound stern, he said, "We'll be going to neither of those places."

"Want to bet?" Now the seductress looked at him. "I'll wear you down."

"Dora, you don't want to give me that great and wonderful gift." Though he'd trade half his soul for it. He could already feel her trembling beneath him, half shy and half eager. "You'll meet your decent, boring man someday. I wouldn't spoil that for anything."

"I've met my man, and he's anything but boring."

"Yes? And what would your family say?"

"My family loves me. More than that, they trust me to make good decisions. You might try the same."

"I'm not a good decision, darling."

"Tell my heart that."

O'Hare only wished he could, and his own along with it.

Chapter Fifteen

"What I think," Dorothea said decidedly, "is that you should lie low for a while. Go underground where no one can find you, till all this dies down."

She eyed O'Hare in an effort to read his mood. The three of them—Ron Murray included—sat round a table in Ron's upstairs quarters, sharing a pot of tea. O'Hare appeared relaxed, sitting with his elbow propped on the table and one leg bent across his other knee. But Dorothea sensed the tension he strove to disguise.

"Will it die down, though?" Ron Murray objected. "The way I see it, there'll be unrest until there's some sort of equality established."

"I want to know how *he* sees it." Dorothea nodded at O'Hare.

His tawny eyes met hers. What did she see there? What had she seen when she told him she loved him? Dismay? Caution? A brief flare of passion?

She feared he'd prove stubborn now—not that he usually did, not stubborn the way she was, anyway. Hare O'Hare didn't indulge in displays of emotion; he just gave that half smile—the one even now curling his lips—and carried on.

But she needed so desperately for him to give in, to be safe. Her fingers tensed around her tea cup. What could she do to convince him?

Softly, he said, "An assassin could find me any day of the week. That's what you're worrying about, isn't it? An assassin? It's no secret who I am, or where I work. Thugs could take me on the street or come here at any time. It's a risk I take for the cause."

The cause. Dammit. She widened her eyes. "I believe in the cause too—you know that. But I don't believe you need be stupid about it."

"Stupid, is it?" He lifted the mobile eyebrows.

"Yes. What happens to the cause if they eliminate you? If they succeed in silencing your voice? These articles I've written have raised feelings to fever pitch. Maybe you don't appreciate how things have changed…"

"Sentiment has changed, yes."

"And along with it, the danger to you. Losing you as leader would set everything back."

"She has a point there," Ron put in.

"So what do you expect me to do? Hide like an infant? Shrink like a coward? I've a life, and a job. We're in the middle of a big installation."

"I don't ask you to lie low for long, just till the immediate furor raised by the series dies down. I handed in the second-last story today. Only one to go. After that, I'll move on to other things—I'll still be speaking for equality, for the Irish and all women, but this strong light won't be shone directly on you. Then you can reemerge."

"It smacks of cowardice, Dora."

"It does not! It smacks of good sense."

"And where, precisely, do you suggest I go to ground?" he asked with an edge.

"I have an idea about that also."

"I thought she might," Ron remarked.

"Listen to this: we can plot out the details of the final interview any time. I thought we might present your views for the future, your vision of what a fair and just Boston might look like. Once we do that, I can write it ahead. You don't need to be here."

"I don't, eh?"

"No. I thought I'd send you to Maine, to the little town where I'm from. I know my friend Josie will let you stay with her and her family. And once I've handed in the last story, I'll join you there for a few days. I can write my next series from anywhere, so long as Mr. Winton gives his approval."

"Whoa." O'Hare held up a hand. "Maine, you say. What in hell would I want to do in Maine?"

He sounded angry, and Ron gave him a sharp glance.

"Lie low, as I've said. Maybe for a week or two."

"Out of the question."

"But I think—"

"No, Dora. The last place on earth I want to be is Maine."

"Why?"

He shook his head, his face closed tight.

"But it's a reasonable plan. You can take the train most of the way and catch a packet boat to…"

"I said no. I'm not leaving here, and I'm not abandoning my responsibilities—or the fight."

Heat rose to Dorothea's head. When she lost her temper, it was quick and fierce. "Let someone else lead the bloody fight for a few days. Are you the only Irish man in Boston?"

"Not by a long chalk. But I've struggled hard to get

115

myself in a position to do some good. You can't expect me to back down just because you fancy—" He waved a hand.

"Now…" Ron attempted to intervene. "Let's not speak in haste, here. Lad, the lady has your welfare at heart."

Close at heart. Dorothea gazed at O'Hare intently. Didn't he realize she couldn't rest with him in danger? That she'd have no peace while he stood in jeopardy?

He visibly strove to compose himself. Whatever else Hare O'Hare might be, he was not a man who flew off the handle easily. "Dora, lass, I do understand your concern. But I can't walk away from this. If I've knocks to take, I'll take them. It won't be the first time."

Panic joined the terror in Dorothea's heart. Would he just dismiss this raging trepidation she felt on his behalf?

She challenged, "Yes, and what if it's the last time?"

He shrugged. "Then I hope I leave this world a bit better than I found it."

Dorothea surged to her feet on a rush of anger—or perhaps it was dismay—and glared at him.

"So you'll throw your life away? Let them win by vanquishing you? And that will advance the cause how? By making you a martyr? I'm surprised. I truly am—I never expected you to behave so stupidly."

He returned her glare with one that glowed like amber. "Well, now you know the truth about me and what to expect—I'm stupid as well as lowborn. Good thing you found out now, eh? A lucky escape."

Dorothea snatched up her hat from the table and slammed it on her head. "Don't say I didn't warn you."

"I'll never be saying that."

"I will write the last piece from my notes, shall I, so you don't have to see me again?"

"You'll do as you wish."

"You're right." She walked to the door that led downstairs. "I absolutely will."

****

"Well, now," Ron said softly after several moments passed and the reverberations from Dorothea's forceful exit died down. "You might have been a little rough with her there."

"No, I wasn't, Ron. I was kind. She's been getting ideas. About me. Best she should lose them now before there's any damage done."

"Heaven forfend that anyone should care about you."

O'Hare looked up sharply, his gaze narrowed on Ron's face. He gave a hard laugh. "No one ever has."

"You have friends."

He did, and good ones, like this man beside him. "I'm not talking about friends. My ma and Gene—growing up with them I always felt like an afterthought. I don't even know why they kept me around. We traveled all over New England before Gene settled in Boston—they could have lost me anywhere."

"You were her son. How could she abandon you?"

O'Hare thought of his ma lying on her deathbed and the look in her eyes. He buried his face in his hands.

"Anyway," Ron went on steadily, "sometimes friends are better than family. In a way they *are* family."

"True."

"So why chase one away? You're whimpering because no one's ever cared for you…"

"Not whimpering, dammit!"

"Sounds like whimpering to me. And here comes somebody tearing herself up because she cares so much—"

"That's just it, Ron. Look at her! Smart, beautiful, with that bright spirit and a heart so full of compassion she'd spill it on one such as me. She deserves the best."

"Reckon she does, when you put it like that. I was going to ask if you've been getting ideas about her. Don't suppose I have to, after that description."

"I've never met anyone like her," O'Hare admitted bleakly. "And I'm fighting all the time to resist. So drop it, will you?"

"Even if I think you're being as stupid as she claims? She's a prize, sure. I see that. But why shouldn't you claim that prize?"

O'Hare lifted his face from his hands. "Oh, yes, because I've so much to offer. The bastard son of a barmaid who drank herself to death, with a ragtag past and a piecemeal education, working as a laborer—"

"A skilled laborer, mind! You've a damn good job."

"And living in a room at the top of a tenement. She says her father's a blacksmith. He'd flatten me with his hammer if she ever took me home. As for what her ma would likely say…"

"She's a grown woman, living and working on her own. Surely it's up to her whom she marries."

"Marries?" Mirroring Dorothea's movement, O'Hare scraped to his feet. "Whoever said anything about marriage?"

Chapter Sixteen

"Miss Sinclair, come in." Montgomery Winton gestured with a peremptory hand for Dorothea to enter his office.

She hesitated at the door; the chief editor wasn't alone. Instead, his son Jeremy accompanied him. Dorothea preferred to continue avoiding the younger Winton, especially today when her feelings still felt raw following yesterday's confrontation with O'Hare. She'd barely slept for reliving it over again and trying unsuccessfully to work through her residual anger.

And hurt. She might as well be honest and admit hurt lay uppermost. She'd thought she meant something to the man—something more than a way to fight his battle.

So she'd been wrong. She needed to pull herself up and get over it. Was she a sniveling child?

When she failed to move, Montgomery Winton gestured still more demandingly. "I hope you've come to hand in the final piece."

Dorothea didn't answer. She clutched the last story of her series in her hands, and even in her estimation it represented a tour-de-force. But now the atmosphere in the room made her feel uncertain.

Plus, she'd put words in Hare O'Hare's mouth, and he really should see the piece before she submitted it. That, though, would mean her meeting with him. The prospect elevated her heartbeat and brought back the anger, along with the hurt. Yet surely she owed him that much?

She stepped into Montgomery Winton's office and shut the door behind her. Something made her say, "The story is roughed out but not quite finished. There are a few facts I need to verify."

Jeremy Winton drawled, "But it goes to press tonight."

"I know that." She jerked her chin. "I was going to ask for more time."

The two men exchanged glances.

"Readers will be expecting the last installment," Winton said.

"So," Jeremy said surprisingly, "if it delays a day, we'll sell more papers. And there's the other story."

"What other story?" Dorothea asked.

Winton ignored her. "I'm not sure I want to run that," he told Jeremy.

"It's front page."

"Unquestionably. But think of the impact if he actually gets taken out."

Jeremy's eyes narrowed. "I hadn't considered that. But it's questionable, surely, to withhold such information?"

"Also problematical to run a story. I must maintain that tip was given to me anonymously." Montgomery Winton showed his teeth in a shark's smile.

"Excuse me, Mr. Winton—about whom are you speaking? And if *who* gets taken out?"

Both men looked at her, and just like that she knew. She might lack her friend Jo's psychic ability to sense trouble, but she possessed something far more acute—intense feelings and an instinct about Hare O'Hare.

She gasped, "Someone's put out a contract on him? Hare O'Hare?"

"The most hated man in Boston," Jeremy pronounced. He nodded at the sheaf of paper in her hands. "Thanks to you."

Winton Senior said, "Your series has stirred up rabid interest. What I'm trying to decide is what would create still more—an exposé of a contract on O'Hare's head, or what will follow when he's eliminated."

Dorothea stared in horror. "Well, of course you have to warn him."

"Not necessarily." Montgomery tapped his chin.

Jeremy took it up. "This information was given to my father in the strictest confidence. Given, in fact, by someone very close to me. That means it can go no further than this room."

"On penalty of you losing your position," Montgomery added darkly.

"But we're talking about a man's life. Ethically…"

"This is the newspaper business, Miss Sinclair. Ethics don't necessarily apply."

"My source," Jeremy told her, "says the assassin means to make a show of it. Everyone knows where Hare O'Hare lives and works. But Irishmen get attacked in this city every day. He'll be taken out in a prominent place—left to make a most effective tableau. His death will be a statement on the part of those who want to keep the Irish down." Jeremy grinned. "A bit like Jesus, really—kill their hero, and they'll truly feel it."

Rage overcame the sickness in Dorothea's belly

and kept her on her feet. "Except, in case you haven't noticed, Christianity's still flourishing, even in Boston. So are you involved in this proposed assassination? You said 'we.' "

Jeremy shot his cuffs. "Not personally, of course. I wouldn't soil my hands with that kind of trash."

"But you're in on it financially."

"I'm not saying that either. But in my opinion, you've done this city a great disservice making a glorious hero out of that ignorant lout, even if it has sold papers."

"An unprecedented number of papers," Montgomery put in.

"But as all too often happens with heroes in real life, he will have to pay the price."

Dorothea turned disbelieving eyes on Montgomery Winton. "Will you just let this happen?"

Montgomery shrugged. "O'Hare's served his purpose, given that's the final story you hold in your hands. I'm inclined to agree with my son; the next story's in the assassination."

Dorothea drew herself up. "And if I take the story of what you've done to the *Herald* or the *Courier*?"

"You wouldn't want to do that, darling. We've indulged you far too much in this—given you fame you don't deserve. At best, you're a so-so writer, but you fixed it so the great hero would speak only to you." Jeremy swept her with his gaze, up and down. "I can only guess how."

"How dare you! And I'm not your darling."

"No, not mine—but I'm beginning to wonder about *his*. The tone of your stories has turned my stomach. It's time for the *Guardian* to return to its idiom. And it will, after your next story runs."

Heat flooded Dorothea's face. "Hate-mongering, you mean. Perhaps I truly should take my final installment elsewhere."

"Miss Sinclair, we have an agreement." Montgomery glared at her. "Surely you don't intend to go back on it?"

"Of course she doesn't, Father," Jeremy answered for her. "She wouldn't be so foolish as to cross us. She knows it isn't safe to cross a man with my connections. She might find O'Hare's not the only one with a contract out on him."

Dorothea recoiled, the sheaf of papers clutched to her chest. For once her thoughts outdistanced her rage.

"No, Mr. Winton, I wouldn't double-cross you. We had an agreement, and I'll abide by it."

"I'm glad to hear that, Miss Sinclair."

"But I did come to tell you the final installment's not quite ready. As I say, I still need to check a few facts."

Winton grunted. "I'll give you the rest of the afternoon." He shot a look at his son. "We'll run the final installment tomorrow. Let O'Hare take his chances."

Jeremy nodded, his gaze never leaving Dorothea.

"Miss Sinclair, I suggest you get to work. I want that copy before you go home tonight, do you understand?"

"Yes, sir."

Dorothea left the office and returned to her desk like a woman in a trance.

She had to leave here now, get to O'Hare, and warn him of the danger in which he stood, despite the way they'd last parted and the hard feelings between them. None of that mattered now. An assassin might lurk anywhere—on a street corner, in an alley. Death might walk into Ron Murray's shop even while Hare worked.

And if she lost Hare O'Hare, she would lose her heart.

But she couldn't leave here immediately and go to him. *Oh, agony!* For Jeremy had emerged from his father's office and now kept an eye on her.

One wrong move and he'd be on her. He might even prevent her going to Hare.

No, she had to play along, somehow come up with the discipline to work on a story already completed, knowing every moment might be the one that ended the life of the man she loved. At the finish of the workday, once she handed in her story, only then could she go to him.

"Dorothea? What's wrong? You look terribly upset."

Molly stood by her desk, having emerged from the typesetting room.

"I'm all right, Molly."

"Are you sure? I saw you come out of Winton's office. Say he never fired you."

"He didn't. Better go back to your job, Moll. I don't want you to get in trouble on my account."

"Are you in trouble?" Molly persisted.

"Dorothea glanced at Jeremy, who still watched her. Fiercely she shook her head.

And knew she lied. Her heart lay in far more peril than she'd ever imagined.

Chapter Seventeen

"I'm sorry, Miss Sinclair, he's not here." Ron Murray frowned at Dorothea in concern. "Left early, he did; had a meeting with someone."

"Who? Where?" Desperation gripped Dorothea's throat so she could barely speak. She'd taken two cabs and run blocks through the gathering dark to reach Ron's shop, only to find her quarry flown. Now her knees threatened to go out from under her.

"Here, sit down." Ron guided her to a chair. "What's the matter?"

"He's in danger. I found out today. Someone's hired an assassin. An assassin, Mr. Murray!"

Ron studied her with emotionless, hazel eyes. "Wouldn't be the first time. He's survived two attempts in the past, plus as many beatings. Put in hospital once. Do you think he knows about this?"

She shook her head. "How could he? I just found out today at the newspaper office. I wanted to come at once but couldn't get away." She shuddered; Jeremy Winton had kept his eye on her all day, till she handed in her story and left in Molly's company. She'd taken a cab home in case he had her followed, waited ten minutes, and taken another to within walking—or running—distance of Ron's shop.

"I have to warn him, Mr. Murray. Do you have any idea where he went?"

"Most likely to Dooley's."

"That's a tavern, isn't it?" She pushed to her feet. "I think I know where it is."

"Miss—you can't go there by yourself. It's a rough place and a dangerous neighborhood."

"He's the one in danger, and better for being warned."

"Well, you'll not go alone. Just let me close up; I'll take you."

"Oh, Mr. Murray, I'd appreciate that."

It seemed to take forever for Ron to shut the shop, interrupted by a customer whom he politely turned away. By the time they left, full dark had fallen. Clouds trailed inland from the ocean like ink.

"How'd you find out about this threat, Miss Sinclair?"

"I heard my employer, Mr. Winton, and his son, Jeremy, talking. They made no secret of it, at least to me."

"Jeremy Winton—he's got a reputation round town, all right. Runs with a wild crowd when he's not chasing women—thugs masquerading as toffs, they are. Word on the street is they've bashed many an Irishman. They like to catch a man when he's on his own, the cowards. Rumor has it they killed at least one."

"I believe it. It seems I've been spending my time in a snake pit, Mr. Murray. You can be sure that's at an end."

"Does that mean you'll be quitting the *Guardian*?"

"Something like that."

Dooley's brimmed with light and sound. A group of what could only be lightskirts stood outside the door with a couple of men. They eyed Dorothea and Ron curiously and called soft taunts.

"You don't belong here, lass."

"Aye—stick to your own patch. We don't need any more competition."

Ron put his arm around Dorothea and ushered her in. She looked around in consternation, fearing she'd never find Hare among the throng that filled the place. A crowded bar occupied one wall, rows of booths the other, with tables—all taken—in between. More groups of people stood about, and a band in the corner competed with dozens of voices to be heard.

"Oh, my," she breathed.

Ron pulled her aside as two men barreled toward them, half angry and half laughing.

"Take it outside, lads!" someone hollered, and hands opened the door for the men as they rolled through. A barmaid passed by, balancing three plates of food, the smell of which reached Dorothea's nostrils and turned her stomach.

She fought back concurrent waves of sickness and panic. "How do we find him?"

"Good question, miss. If he's here to meet someone, he won't be standing out in the open. Come along."

Ron guided Dorothea to the left side of the room, edging his way through the crowd. The booths, ill-lit, looked like smoky caves where patrons—men and women together or just groups of men with their heads close—glanced up to glare at them. One couple, both on the same side of the table, occupied themselves with something beyond conversation and didn't look up at all. Dorothea determinedly turned her eyes away.

But a new thought occurred to her: what if Hare

had come here not to meet a man but a woman? What if she happened upon him in just such a clench with his hand down some female's bodice? She didn't know what he got up to in his free time. And he didn't belong to her.

Much as she might want him to.

That thought startled her, so she barely noticed when Ron grunted, "There."

Still with his arm around Dorothea's shoulders, he guided her to the very back of the room, opposite the band, where gloom hung thickest. Here, Dorothea realized, a patron stood the least chance of being seen—or overheard.

And there sat a man with copper curls that looked bright even in the poor light, speaking earnestly with another man parked across from him. They both looked up when Ron paused beside their booth, the stranger with a forbidding glare and Hare O'Hare with astonishment.

He came to his feet as if drawn by force, and his tawny eyes went wide. "Dora?"

She could barely hear him. The band had broken into a lilting tune that had several couples on the packed floor, swaying.

O'Hare leaned close enough for her to smell the ale on his breath. "What are you doing here?"

She placed her mouth at his ear in turn. "I had to see you. To warn you. Mr. Murray was kind enough—"

Hare nodded at Ron. The stranger got to his feet abruptly and shot Dorothea a second dark look. "I'm off."

Without another word, he melted into the crowd. Ron herded Dorothea into his seat; her knees collapsed, and she subsided behind the man's half-drunk mug of black ale.

"I'll leave her with you," Ron told Hare and moved away also before Dorothea could protest.

Hare returned to his seat, and they regarded one another. A thousand emotions tumbled through Dorothea's breast, and she saw most of them reflected in Hare's eyes. They'd last parted in anger, but she found she didn't care about that. She reached across the table and grasped his hands. He turned his fingers to grip hers, hard and strong.

"You shouldn't be here."

"I had to see you."

"Another warning?" he asked, leaning close across the table so she could hear him. "Did we not quarrel over the last?"

"We did. As you can see, that did not serve to discourage me. Because here I am."

"Here you are," he echoed.

"Whether you like it or not." Sudden tears filled her eyes. "You're a hardheaded Irishman, and you drive me to distraction, but I—" She had no words for the rest. Instead, she leaned still closer and kissed him, letting her emotions do the talking in a gesture filled with her fear for him, and her devotion.

For an instant his lips, against hers, remained merely acquiescent. Then he began to participate enthusiastically, his lips molding to hers, wooing and coaxing them apart. Time stood still and even the tumult around them faded away as Dorothea tasted him: his warmth and the spice of ale, the passion and the essence that was his alone.

Both his hands came up and cradled her face. He

broke the kiss but didn't release her. Staring into her eyes, he breathed, "Dora, Dora, by God, what am I to do with you?"

She could think of several things, all of which shocked her. She dismissed her shock as irrelevant. She wanted this man, wanted his company, his attention, his conversation, and his touch. His presence in her life made her understand so many truths, including the fact that men and women were halves of the same whole.

And he—with his warm hands, guarded eyes, and courageous heart—had been made for her. She didn't understand how, or why—just that he was her other half.

"Love me?" she suggested, calling upon every shred of courage.

He shook his head, and emotion brimmed in his eyes. She thought for an instant he meant to push her away even as he had in Ron Murray's quarters. Instead he asked, "How can I do anything else?"

He kissed her then, her face still fast between his hands, making a thorough job of it and setting Dorothea's blood alight. A joyful song started up in her mind. He loved her. He'd as much as admitted it. His heart was hers, the one prize she wanted in all the world.

This time when the kiss ended she gazed into his eyes and said raggedly, "Take me somewhere. Your room."

"Dora, no."

"Do you really intend to try arguing with me again?"

He laughed. "No."

"We need some place quiet where we can talk."

"Talk, is it?" Devilment leaped in his eyes. "That kiss did not taste like talking."

She gifted him with another, quick and hard—a promise. "But I came here with a warning for you. Listen. I discovered today your enemies have hired an assassin. There's a price on your head."

"How did you find this out?"

"At the newspaper office. I came as soon as I could…"

"Hush." He held up a hand, even though, close as they were, no one could possibly overhear them. "You're right, we cannot talk here."

"Where will we go? Not Mrs. Bennett's."

"No. Come on."

He took her by the hand, pulled her from the booth, and headed for the door. Halfway there, they were jostled by two men; just as Ron had, Hare wrapped his arm around her shoulders.

She pressed into his warmth. This felt nothing like contact with Ron Murray. Instead, Hare's heat and strength started a fire low down in her belly and threatened to melt the last of her resistance.

She'd come to warn him of danger. But she suspected her danger lay in his arms.

Chapter Eighteen

"Perhaps we should hire a cab."

Dora Sinclair stood on the street corner, still within the circle of Hare's arm, looking wonderfully disheveled. He'd kissed her outside Dooley's with the lightskirts hooting in approval, kissed her on the curb while they waited for a cart to lumber past, and again when they reached the other side of the street. Now her hat sat askew on her head and her hair—that glorious mane through which his hands had plowed—tumbled down her neck.

And what the hell had come over him, planting kisses on Dorothea Sinclair? He'd worked so hard to resist the temptation she represented, if only for her sake. Why fall victim now?

Maybe it was due to how injured he'd felt at parting with her in anger, last time they met. Maybe it was her sweetness, the innocence mixed with sheer strength he tasted in her kisses. Maybe it was the way she looked at him, enough to warm his soul.

He tossed her a glance of amusement. "No one hires a cab in this neighborhood, sweetheart. Where do you think we are?"

"Sweetheart?" She pressed closer to him. "Say that again."

"Sweetheart." He accompanied the word with still another kiss, and she sagged against him.

He slid his hands around her waist and, greatly daring, still lower. She pressed a pertinent area of her body against a pertinent part of his.

"Behave yourself, Miss Sinclair."

"I don't feel like behaving myself." To prove it she slid her tongue into his mouth, testing the waters, so to speak, and melting his bones in the process. How could such an innocent stoke such a fire?

"Hey! Irishman!"

The call came from down the street and spun Hare's head around. He saw three shadowy figures— no, four—surrounded by the mist that swirled over the cobbles. Ah, damnation. Only see where being distracted had got him.

"Who's that?" Dora breathed.

"Trouble."

"Who—"

"Thugs. Irish head-bashers. Come on."

"But I…"

"Irishman! Want to share your doxy? Or should we just take what we want?"

"Run."

Putting his own word into action, he took to his heels, Dora's hand caught in his.

He ran the way a fox does from the hounds. A similar result would be forthcoming, he knew, if they caught him; hounds tore the fox—or in his case the hare—to pieces. What would then happen to Dora, he shuddered to think.

They thought her his doxy and him impatient for a kiss and cuddle on the street corner. They'd beat him to a pulp—oh, he'd fight, but there were four of them, doubtless with coshes, and he'd been there before.

They'd use her harshly, and Dora, as he knew full well, a tender, untried maiden.

He'd die first. But before that they'd have to catch him. He knew the area—as interlopers, they probably didn't. He'd seen their ilk many times, upper-class young bloods out on a bender turned nasty. That made an advantage; the fact that Dora couldn't run very fast in her long skirts made a disadvantage.

Though he must admit, as they rounded a corner and plunged into a dark alley, she didn't do badly for herself. With her free hand she'd hiked up her skirts, and her neat little boots flashed in the gloom.

"What—?" She tried to speak again when they gained the relative shelter of the alley.

"Quiet. Sound carries. Come on."

Not allowing her to rest, he exited the alley at the other end and pelted off down another street, nearly deserted. A district of humble businesses and storage buildings, the area offered no acquaintance he might knock up for refuge, and few places to hide. He tried wildly to think. Most sanctuary lay too far away, all but one.

He heard the echoing pound of footsteps behind him, and the thugs appeared from the alley. They called again, their voices taunts that made Dora catch her breath.

"Hare? What will they do to us?"

"Don't ask."

Round yet another corner and down the street. He didn't want to get trapped, and his thoughts ran ahead, trying to probe the darkness. Was there a way to double back to the light, the sound—the Irishness of Dooley's? Not without getting intercepted.

The thugs called again—they sounded no closer. Dora began to flag, her breath coming ragged and her hand dragging at his.

"Just a bit farther," he promised and pulled her between two buildings. Had they been seen? He hoped not; shadows lay deep on this side of the street. Their pursuers might think they'd gone straight on.

Not waiting to find out, he drew Dora through the narrow, malodorous passage and into a yard littered with trash, where he drew her against a wall and shielded her body with his.

"Hush now," he breathed into her ear, "like a mouse."

Bless her, she complied, caught her breath, and tried to silence it. The night grew quiet around them, only a slight breeze sighing around the stones of the buildings. Something moved close beside them, and Dora tensed; Hare could feel her heart beating against his chest, so close were they.

"Tomcat," he breathed.

She sagged, and her arms stole around him; her head came to rest on his shoulder.

His world shifted; all at once nothing remained the same. Danger transformed to tenderness and even the nature of the darkness seemed different, a haven where they might be together. Any place became bliss, with Dorothea Sinclair in his arms.

And that frightened him more than the thugs chasing them down; a deep, primal terror started. He'd striven his whole life to keep from needing anyone— not his ma, certainly not Gene, who made a poor excuse for a pa. Not his non-existent family. He might care for his friends, yes, but their lives didn't affect his.

Now, though, he held his well-being in his arms. Perilous!

"Are they gone?"

She barely breathed the words into his ear, but they jogged him back to reality.

"Must be. You all right?"

"Yes. What—?"

"Come along. Carefully now."

They went over a fence at the rear of the property, with Hare lifting her before swinging himself across. They traversed another network of streets before she asked, "Are we safe now?"

"They'll be watching for us yet. We'll have to wait it out till they tire and go for another drink. Here."

He paused at the door of a dark building and fumbled with the lock. When the door opened, they stumbled in.

"Where are we?"

"I used to work here. Ran errands for the man who operated the shop. He lived upstairs." As he spoke he drew her up a narrow flight of wooden steps and through another door at the top—to safety, he hoped.

There, at last, he let go of her hand.

"What happened to him?"

"Dead. The shop's been abandoned. We can rest here, I hope."

"Who were those men? Assassins?"

"Assassins! No, just young bloods out on a lark."

"A lark! They wanted to beat you up."

"Yes."

He could feel her contemplating that. Very little light penetrated the dirt on the windows, but he didn't need light to read what went on in her quick mind.

Yet she surprised him when she said, "I lost my hat somewhere back there. I don't think you can rescue this one."

All at once she wept, both hands raised to her cheeks—a reaction to the terror. He took her in his arms and drew her close against him once more, where she belonged.

"Ah, lass, don't cry. I'll buy you another hat."

"That would be f-foolish, spending good money on a hat when there are families like the Gallaghers who need so much help. Only, that makes two hats. Jo made them both for me, and I loved them."

What could he say to such beautiful logic and illogic at once? He didn't try to find words, just slid his lips over her temple to the corner of her eye and down her cheek, gathering the tears.

Her mouth found his, and passion flared bright enough to sear him. Damn, if time didn't stop again, performing that trick he found so terrifying.

He no longer knew where her mouth began and his ended; their bodies had become one, and their hearts—but no, he couldn't give her his heart even though it starved for what she held out to him.

The kiss ended at last, and she told him, "I want you, Hare O'Hare."

"What?"

"Want you the way a woman wants a man. Do I have to put it any more clearly?"

She did not. Her lips spoke clearly enough as she brushed them across his, as did her body trembling in his arms.

He drew a shuddering breath. "I need to take you home."

"Not yet. It won't be safe." She kissed him long and lingeringly.

It wasn't safe here. Every instinct told him so. Gently, he cradled her between his hands and eased away, just a breath. "You think I'd ruin you? You suppose I care so little as that?"

"Hmm, a man of honor."

She tried to kiss him again, but he held her off.

"What is it, Hare O'Hare? Do you not fancy me?"

Was that a wicked gleam he caught in her eyes? Maybe not so innocent as she seemed. Surely, pressed so close against him, she could feel his desire.

"I will tell you the truth, Dora Sinclair. I want you; I'm fair aflame with it. But I want to protect you even more. Which is why we'll wait another ten minutes till those hounds tire—and then I'll take you home."

"Can't," she whispered.

"Beg pardon?"

"I've missed my curfew."

"Knock at the door; sure the old woman will let you in."

"She won't. Once Mrs. Bennett locks the door, she absolutely will not open it again."

"Fine, that. What does she expect you to do?"

"Fortunately, I'm in the arms of a gentleman who will look after me till morning. Take me to your room."

"There? I hardly think so—the place is not fit. And a gentleman would do no such thing."

She sighed with what sounded suspiciously like contentment. "We'll have to stay here then."

"Eh?"

She leaned still closer, seduction in a prim, proper package. "Here. Together. Till morning."

Chapter Nineteen

"Jesus, Dora—show a bit of mercy, will you not?" The request came from Hare's throat like a groan.

Dorothea didn't feel particularly merciful. A host of other feelings burgeoned through her—victorious gladness at being in his arms, frighteningly deep certainty, and desire hot enough to set the room ablaze. If he thought she'd let go of him now for something as weak-willed as mercy...

Perhaps sensing her thoughts, he went on, "What about your reputation?"

"What about it? We're alone here. No one will ever know."

"I'll know. By God, you'll know. God and all the angels—"

"Don't bring them into it." She strained to see what lay in his eyes. "What's so terrible about it? Is it wrong to be with the man I love? Isn't that the purpose for which nature made us?"

"You don't love me."

"That again? Do you still mean to try and tell me how I feel? Haven't you learned better?"

He closed his eyes, a man in pain.

"I love you, Hare O'Hare."

"You barely know me. That's not even my true name."

"Then tell me." She whispered it, and he opened

139

his eyes to gaze into hers. "Give me all you are, here and now."

"Seductress. Not bad enough you're clever and beautiful. You have to—" He broke off.

"Have to what?"

"Make me believe you want me also."

"Want you? I'm about to fall on you like a ravening beast."

That coaxed a surprised laugh from him. "Dora."

"Say my name again; I love how you say it."

"Dora."

"Speak it in my ear. In the dark, over and over again."

He placed his lips against her ear, and she shivered delightedly.

"Oh, yes. Hare O'Hare—by whatever name—I do love you. What's more, I believe you love me, too."

"Oh, God …"

"Stop praying and do something about it."

This time, before the kiss ended she had her hands up inside his shirt. Smooth, warm skin and hard muscle met her fingertips, and a line of hair that made her weak in the knees. She wanted that body against hers so much she could barely think.

"Touch me, too," she requested wildly. He hadn't denied he loved her. Coming from this man, it equaled a declaration. "Why don't you touch me?"

"I'm holding back my desire by a string. A shredded string, at that."

"Well, let go."

She kissed his throat, moved her mouth down to his collarbone, leaving kisses all the way. The buttons of his shirt yielded to her fingers one by one. He stiffened like a stallion.

Suddenly she felt his fingers in her hair. It had mostly tumbled down during their flight; now he freed the rest of it, plunged his hands into the heavy tresses, drew her head back, and looked into her eyes.

For an instant she saw his soul—wild and hungry, and so loving it stole her breath. She distinctly felt his hard-held control snap before his passion rushed her in a kiss that claimed her body and spirit.

She forgot who she was, then, and who he was— surely they were meant to be one, sharing breath, being, and sensation. If they melded together now in the act she'd never yet completed, making one flesh, that could only be right. For the flesh must follow the heart which she presented to him in a glorious burst of gladness.

"Dora, Dora." He sounded broken when he ended the kiss only to shower smaller caresses across her face. "Beautiful. You're so beautiful."

Victorious delight pierced her even as her heart told her full well this glorious moment had nothing to do with how either of them looked. Rather, they'd been fashioned by nature long ago to fill some deep need in each other. How miraculous they had come together at all.

"Bed," she breathed.

That startled him. "Eh?"

"I think I saw a bed in the corner."

"Dora, it will be all full of mice."

"I don't care. Go lock the door. Does it lock?"

He turned from her without a word, though she felt the protests gathering in him. She'd have some fancy talking to do yet, if she meant to have him this night.

She surveyed the room. Her eyes had now adjusted

to the dim light, and she saw dust lay thick everywhere; an abandoned table, devoid of chairs, stood by the single dirt-streaked window. Several crates lay about and, strangely, a frying pan. The bare mattress in the corner had slid halfway off the bedstead. The room felt cold.

This didn't match how she'd imagined losing her virginity—if she'd imagined it at all. That had never been more than a far distant, hazy possibility. She'd lived her life in a place of intellect; any man who approached that high altar would have had to win her, and not easily.

Now she used her knees to nudge the mattress back onto the frame and contemplated, truly contemplated, what she was doing. She intended to present herself on that altar to a man who fitted none of her preconceived notions.

And who yet fit her like a second skin. She wanted to be inside that skin with him, wanted it more than she'd ever imagined wanting anything.

Who knew passion had a force of its own? Who knew she'd succumb to it like a frail blade of grass before a scythe?

She began unbuttoning her shirtwaist with hands steady and certain. Hare returned from the door and wrapped his arms around her from behind, covered her hands with his.

"Don't. I won't have you here. It's—it's sordid."

She sagged against him. Warmth, belonging. Rightness.

"No place can be sordid if I'm with you."

"This is the very definition of sordid." He drew a breath. "Dora, I can't let you give yourself to me. I'm the son of a whore and a—well, I don't even know what he was."

She turned in his arms, her bodice open—an invitation. "I don't know what he was either, but I know what you are—a fine man. I'd be honored to give myself to you. Here, now."

"Madness." But as if unable to help himself he slid his hands up to cup her breasts, first from the outside, and when she did not protest, very gently inside the gaping fabric, his rough palms against her skin.

Dora's knees nearly failed her. More wonder than demand filled his touch; he caressed her carefully, the way he might handle glass.

She whispered, "No one will come to bother us, because no one knows we're here—just you and me. Nothing can take this from us." She brushed her lips across his even as she arched into his palms. "Do you trust me?"

"Oh, yes."

"Then tell me your name—your real given name— so I might speak it when you claim me."

"Timothy."

"Timothy, I pledge to you my heart, and I give to you all I am—"

"No. Stop. I—"

"Do you mean to spoil this moment by beginning that again? Truly? With your hands inside my bodice and the whole night ahead, filled only with time?"

"And if I leave you with a child this night, beautiful Dora? It happens. Unwanted children are made in stolen moments of passion; no one knows that better than me."

She caught his face between her hands. "What

makes you think I wouldn't want your child? I want all of you."

"No, Dora. I care too much for that. I'll hold you all this night long; I'll kiss you and touch you. I'll not create another such as myself."

Tears flooded her eyes. Could she have found a finer man? "I love you, Timothy. Oh, how I love you." And she drew him down on the bed.

Chapter Twenty

Somewhere in the distance a dog barked and roused Hare from a light doze. His thoughts oriented with an almost audible click; he lay on the dusty mattress in Mick O'Sheedy's abandoned quarters.

With a naked Dorothea Sinclair in his arms. Truth be told, they both lay stark naked, she cuddled into him for warmth—or for another purpose that fair stole his breath away.

He could no longer doubt she loved him. She'd shed her clothing willingly and coaxed him from his, her eyes going round when she caught her first sight of his arousal. He'd not used that—despite the temptation—to steal her virginity, but he'd made great inroads upon it using the rest of his body, his mouth and hands.

He'd sooner die than do anything to harm her.

He lay now staring at the shadowed ceiling and contemplated that fact. He could no longer deny the truth; he loved Dora Sinclair. God help him. God help her. He was the last person she needed in her life, poor lass. Yet here they lay, cleaved together as tightly as two people who hadn't actually completed the act could be, and his heart aching as if it had been shredded.

He'd done his best to provide her the satisfaction she craved without damaging her. He knew enough about women to accomplish that, and his satisfaction be damned. He could sacrifice that for her. He would sacrifice anything.

His arms tightened around her involuntarily, and she stirred against his shoulder. They'd covered themselves with their clothing; her blouse lay across her upper body, only one shoulder peeking out—and that wealth of black hair spilling everywhere.

"Umm." She pressed her lips to his neck, and his pulse leaped impossibly. "Say it's not morning."

"It's not morning."

"Good, because I don't want this night to end."

If only. Reality seemed so far away at this moment he might almost pretend it didn't exist. Almost.

She stretched atop his body, and his poor, disappointed member sprang to life once more. She'd be the death of him…and he'd enjoy it.

"We need to talk."

"Talk, is it? Beautiful lass, this is no time for talking." He kissed her, unable to prevent that either, and she opened to him like a flower, lips and thighs. She learned quickly, did the clever Miss Sinclair.

"No, but this is no time for kissing, either." She belied her words by showering him with little kisses on his chin, neck, and chest.

"Lass, I think I've finally found something you like better than talking."

She laughed and wiggled, affording his lips access to her breast. "Oh, yes."

He laughed too. Who would have thought— laughing in bed with a woman?

But he drew her back down under the makeshift covers determinedly. "Listen to me. This here—this night—it's a time apart, understand? A kind of

146

aberration."

"That's a big word for you to know," she teased, refusing to take him seriously yet.

"I read, don't I?"

"You are most frightfully clever. And principled, even if not what I might ever have imagined for myself…"

Not what he would have imagined for her, either.

"But that just goes to show, life often knows what we need better than we do and writes far more romantic stories. Why, my best friend Jo met her future husband when she was still a slave. Chance brought them together, and she says it was like an irresistible force pulling at her till she found her way home to his arms."

"A slave, was she?"

"Yes, and it was that way for us, wasn't it? It seemed like chance, the wind blowing my hat off my head, yet it wasn't. I couldn't pen a story as beautiful as this."

Lying on a wreck of a mattress in a derelict hovel, and she called it beautiful. He swallowed hard and croaked, "No?"

"No, and do you know what, Timothy?"

"What, lovely Dora?"

"I think I loved you from that very first minute—which just proves there are moments in time when everything pauses and begins to turn in a new direction. That was one. So is this."

Something within him melted; a wall of ice he'd kept in place around his heart for years warmed and fell away. But he said, "Don't go putting me on any pedestals."

"You needn't worry, Timothy. I'm a realist."

"You?" There in the dark he nearly hooted.

"A pedestal's a lonely place. Anyway, I know you have faults—so do I. Everybody does."

"Oh?"

She stretched against him again, rubbing like a cat. "But I'm willing to live with your faults if you'll live with mine. That's what marriage is, right? A kind of bargain. So long as it's a fair bargain on both sides, it works."

His newfound euphoria drained away. "Marriage? Who said anything about…"

"Do we have to say it? Isn't it the natural next step? I'll ask you properly, if you like. Timothy, will you marry me? As soon as possible, so your darned scruples won't be in our way."

"Whoa, lass."

"Because I'll never love anyone else the way I love you. Never."

His poor heart, in a state of flux to rival that of another organ lower down, promptly melted all over again. He cautioned, "Forever's a long time." He knew few people who accomplished "forever," who fell in love—this kind of overwhelming love—and kept it alive. He supposed his ma must have loved Gene that way once. Or maybe not.

This woman in his arms could make him believe damn near anything, even that he might live this dream she wove.

She whispered, "I'm glad forever's a long time—it can't be long enough, with you."

He kissed her, and things grew heated once again. For a while the only sounds were desperate breathing and wordless entreaties. This time his control wavered;

he spilled himself on her thighs there in the cold room, and they held each other like children, he with his hands in her hair, she with her fingers caressing his skin.

"Oh, God, Dora. Oh, God." He didn't want to need her, didn't want to need anyone this much. He'd worked so hard on needing nothing.

She stroked his face with tenderness that went right through him. "You haven't answered my question."

"Still talking? Woman, what does it take to distract you?"

She laughed but persisted, "Will you marry me?"

He stilled. "If I mean to prove my feelings for you, I must say no."

"Tim—"

"Before you start to protest, let me tell you why." Maybe he could convince himself along with her. "You deserve the world, with a man who can give you a comfortable life, provide for you and the children you'll have some day. I'm thinking you will want children, won't you?"

"I want your children."

He tried to ignore the way that made him feel. "What if we did wed? Hare O'Hare and the reporter who wrote about him—for it would get out. I'm surprised it hasn't already. You think we were in danger tonight? That I'm in peril now with a contract out on me? I'd be pulling you right into it, and I refuse to do that."

He rushed on before she could speak. "And let's consider you taking me home—a fine joke, that. You don't even know what my surname is."

"Then tell me."

He considered it: born Grier to his unwed mother, he'd lived most of his life under the name of Browne after she took Eugene's surname. If his ma could be believed—and he thought what she'd told him on her deathbed must be truth—the man who'd fathered him had been called O'Shea. He felt he had little true claim to any of those names more than to the identity of Hare O'Hare the fighter, the crusader.

But this woman lying in his arms deserved something better than the half-truth of a chosen name.

Softly he said, "I can't tell you, and I can't marry you, Dora. Don't ask me for something I'm unable to give."

He expected her to storm and weep—many women would. Being Dora Sinclair, she matter-of-factly persuaded, "You say that now, but fair warning: I'll talk you round. It's just a matter of time. And after all, I don't want anyone but you, so it doesn't matter what you're called. I want you, not your name."

"Lass…"

"You'll see the truth eventually. We need to be together. There's no other course for us, and arguing it is mere furor. As for the trouble we're in—eventually that must be resolved too, right? Meanwhile, I think we should go to the police—most of them are Irish anyway—and tell them someone's put a price on your life. I'll report what I heard the Wintons say. Let Boston's finest protect you. Once that's in the works, I want to take you to Maine. I know you refused before and got upset about it, but just listen. It will give the police time to investigate while you're safe elsewhere."

She paused and peered into his face. "You're not going to grow angry with me, are you?"

"I never want to grow angry with you. But…"

"Good. I want you to meet my family anyway. Again, that's the logical next step. We can stay a week, maybe two."

"I'm not going to Maine."

"Why not? You'll love it there. Come to think of it, maybe we can get married there. My mother and Jo will want to get started on a wedding dress."

He drew a breath. "I'm not going back to Maine, lass."

" 'Back'?"

"I was born there."

"Were you! Well, our story just keeps getting more and more remarkable, doesn't it? Where are you from?"

"Some little town—you'll not have heard of it. I'm not sure I even remember the name. I was no more than three when we left."

"Then there can't be any bad memories for you. And we can make new memories together—all good ones." She kissed him softly there in the dark. "And I promise we'll burn all the bad ones away."

Chapter Twenty-One

Hare whistled under his breath softly as he headed for Dooley's in the new, soft dark. He'd had a message asking him to meet one of the lads there to discuss the threat of job cuts on the docks, and he knew he should be concentrating on what steps they might take to alleviate the ensuing want. Trouble was, he had a bad want of his own, and it went by the name of Dorothea Sinclair.

All day long, as he worked at Ron's, he'd been unable to chase her from his mind. He wished he were going to see her now, not heading for the noise and confusion at Dooley's once again. He found a rare kind of peace in Dora's company, an ease he couldn't remember ever having known. Addictive as strong Irish whiskey was the fine Miss Dorothea, and she clouded his mind almost as powerfully.

How many times this day had he relived their moments together up in the haven of the filthy quarters above the old shop? Her soft words, her trusting movements… She thought she wanted to marry him, by God. And he—

The sudden scuff of a footstep on his heel caused him to pause and spin around. So distracted had he been by his thoughts of Dorothea, he'd abandoned his usual caution and taken to the shadowed side of the street, and a street nearly abandoned, at that.

Except for this man behind him. And the other moving in all too swiftly from the left. And the third whose breath he could now virtually feel on the back of his neck.

He swore in a groan, cursing his own carelessness, and tensed, realizing his danger all too late. The man directly in front of him pulled a cosh from his pocket and smiled like a shark.

"O'Hare, I presume?" he asked.

Oh, Dora, oh, Dora, his mind screamed, and he went in fighting.

****

"Miss Sinclair," Mrs. Bennett said haughtily and with obvious disapproval, "there's a man at the door asking to see you. He seems quite…desperate."

Dora's heart leaped. Could it be Timothy? She hadn't seen him since two nights ago—or rather two mornings ago when they'd parted following their life-changing hours together.

Mrs. Bennett's attitude toward Dorothea had been scathing since her missed curfew. Now she sniffed, "This is not the sort of person I appreciate having at my door. Irish."

Dorothea leaped to her feet, her pen slipping from her hand. "I'll come at once."

Her heart sped as she followed Mrs. Bennett down the steep stairs from her room. Other girls stared as she went by; some lingered in the dining room after supper, sharing a cup of tea.

Mrs. Bennett had shut her caller outside. Dorothea hauled the door open and beheld not Hare but Terry Gallagher.

The last person she'd expected to see.

"Mr. Gallagher!" she exclaimed.

Mrs. Bennet hadn't lied; Terry Gallagher looked frantic. Cold descended over Dorothea like a bucket of icy water; even before she asked, she knew the truth. "What's happened?"

"It's Hare O'Hare, miss. He was found in a gutter by some lads, not far from Dooley's. Must have been on his way there after work. One of the lads recognized him and came to me."

Dorothea gripped the edge of the door as her heart plummeted. "Not—he's not…"

"He's alive. Barely. We took him back to Ron's shop. Ron said I should come for you."

Dorothea's legs threatened to fail her; no time for that now. She had to be strong.

She spoke but two words to Terry. "Take me."

She hurried out without her coat and with all the boarders staring. Through the deepening dark, they ran till the breath seared her lungs and her steps slowed involuntarily. Only once before had she ever run like this, with such desperation.

Now a litany pounded through her mind with every step: *Let him be alive; let him be alive.*

At last Terry paused on a corner, nearly as out of breath as Dorothea. "There."

Lights blazed in Ron's shop even though the surrounding businesses stood dark. The door, half open, emitted a spear of gold, and light shone from the upstairs windows.

"Come on," Terry Gallagher urged.

Dorothea crossed the last distance without feeling her feet touch the ground. In the shop stood three men she didn't know; all wore workmen's clothes and had hangdog faces, their hats in their hands. Upstairs, in the rooms where they'd so lately met together, Ron stood beside what must be his bed. Stretched on the bed…

He looked dead. In that instant, Dorothea believed she'd come too late, and her heart broke apart in her chest, a distinct, shattering pain. The blood drained from her face, and she began to fall.

Ron reached for her. "No, miss—Dorothea, he lives."

"God, are you sure?" She'd never seen anyone— not even the dead—who looked more dead. His face had paled to stark white where it had not swelled or showed red abrasions. He'd been beaten mercilessly; blood flowed from a severe cut on his forehead, and the pillow below his head had turned crimson.

Blood flowed. Yes, he lived still.

"Oh, thank heaven." She stumbled forward and sat on the edge of the bed before taking both Hare's hands in hers. He felt so cold she once more doubted the evidence of her eyes.

"You say he was found near Dooley's?" In her head, Dorothea heard again the words Jeremy Winton had spoken in his father's office: *My source says the assassin means to make a show of it… He'll be taken out in a prominent place.*

"He said nothing about heading for Dooley's when he left here." Ron breathed the words, horror evident in his voice.

"The lads who found him thought him dead. One of them ran for me, and I called some mates—we brought him here, since it was closer than his place, and safer." Terry cleared his throat. "Is it true what I hear— someone's put a price on his life?"

"Yes." And probably believed they'd be paying out now. "You've called a doctor?"

"Aye—one of the lads went." Humbly, Terry added, "But I've no money to pay him."

"I'll pay," Ron said.

"'Tis only Dr. Liffey will come. 'Twill take a while for him to get here."

Dorothea caressed Hare's face, noted the utter stillness of the copper-brown lashes on his cheeks. "Has he regained consciousness at all?"

"No, miss. The back of his head's a right mess. 'Tis clear they bashed it into the brick wall there before they left him."

Ron pushed closer. "Miss Dorothea, it looks bad. You'd best be prepared to lose him."

"I will not!"

"These bashers—they know their work, especially when they're looking to collect. Only the fact that he's so strong is keeping him alive now."

Dorothea gripped Hare's fingers more tightly. She saw his hands were a mess, all the knuckles split and splashed with blood. He'd fought back, certainly, as best he could.

"Bring me some water and cloths, if you have them," she begged Ron. "I'm not waiting for the doctor."

She'd often enough watched her mother patch up her brothers, who constantly got into scrapes. Nothing like this, of course—the worst they suffered was the odd laceration or broken bone. She'd also watched her mother treat her father once after he suffered a bad burn at the forge, and that had been grisly. But again, nothing like this.

Carefully, she washed the abrasions on Hare's face and tried to persuade the deep cut at his hairline to close, even while blood from his injured skull continued to soak the pillow. She dared not touch his head. She bathed his poor hands and unbuttoned his ruined shirt to find more abrasions covering his chest. He'd have broken ribs there, at the very least.

When she'd done all she could, she covered him with a blanket and sat praying for the doctor to come. Throughout all her ministrations, Hare had not opened his eyes or stirred a muscle, and fear closed her throat.

What felt like an eternity crawled by—in truth it could not have been more than an hour. She thought about what likely would have happened had the lads who'd discovered him on the side of the street failed to do so, and anger combined with the terror in her heart.

Not fair, not fair! They'd just found one another, she'd spent but one night in his arms. And the two of them together had a whole, beautiful story to write.

She'd be damned if she'd lose him.

She could hear the men downstairs speaking in hushed voices and Ron's harsh breathing from where he stood by the door. She thought quite clearly: *If his life ends here in this room tonight, mine does also. I won't give up. I won't, I won't...*

The doctor came at last, with a bustle and clatter up the stairs. A younger man than Dorothea expected, he had a face like the map of Ireland and a reddened nose that argued drink might be his vice. He gave Dorothea a sharp look before focusing on his patient.

"Aye, that's Hare O'Hare, right enough. The lad said so, but I thought him mistaken. Jaysus, Mary, and Joseph, they did a brutal job on him, didn't they?"

"Can you save him?"

"That remains to be seen." He gave her another look, this one scathing. "I was not aware this man's married."

"He's not. I'm not…"

"Then you don't belong here. Go off downstairs now, like a good lass, and let me do my work."

"I'm not leaving him. So you can get on with doing your work in spite of me."

Dr. Liffey grunted. "At least give me some elbow room."

Dorothea shifted away, not far. Dr. Liffey barked at Ron, "Well, help me, man. We'll have to shift him."

The ensuing moments would have reduced Dorothea to tears had she not believed weeping would make Dr. Liffey order her from the room. The man possessed a terrible bedside manner and very little patience, but Dorothea could find no fault with his gentle hands when he set to examining Hare's wounds. He swore in a steady stream while he worked, not quite under his breath.

By the time he finished, all three of them—he, Ron, and Dorothea—sweated. O'Hare still lay inert and cold as a corpse.

Dr. Liffey straightened and looked at both of them. "Who's paying me? That's the one to whom I'll speak."

Ron shot Dorothea a helpless look. She hauled herself together.

"Me. I am." Did she have enough money? Cursed if she cared.

"If he makes it to morning, he may live. He has a broken cheekbone, a dislocated shoulder which I've put back into place, and at least three broken ribs. The angels were with him—none penetrated his lung. It's the head injuries that worry me."

"Injuries?" *Plural.*

"Skull was smashed against something hard, and repeatedly. Broke like an egg. There'll be swelling. Merciful thing is he'll probably go in his sleep."

Dorothea swallowed convulsively. "There must be something we can do."

"Stay with him." Dr. Liffey raked her with a hard glance. "If you love him, hold onto him. He seems to have a lot of fight."

"Doctor," Ron got out, "what odds do you give him?"

"Of making morning? Twenty percent."

The doctor began repacking his bag, while Ron and Dorothea stared at one another in horror.

"You can't leave," Dorothea squeaked then.

"I certainly can't stay."

"What if he takes a turn for the worse?"

"If he turns worse than that, he'll surely be dead." Dr. Liffey held out a red-stained hand. "My fee's two dollars."

"I'm sorry, I ran out without my purse. Ron—?"

Ron Murray paid the doctor in silence and saw him to the door. By the time he returned, Dorothea sat once more on the edge of the bed, wracked by sobs.

"Here, girl—he's not gone yet. You heard what the doc said—he has a lot of fight."

Dorothea found it impossible to speak.

"Here, you sit with him. Talk to him, like. You want me to send back to your rooming house for anything?"

Numbly, Dorothea shook her head. "I'll pay you

back for the doctor's fee, Mr. Murray."

"Don't spare a thought for that. It's only money. You just sit there and keep holding onto him, girl. Don't let go."

"I will." What more could she do?

Chapter Twenty-Two

When the gray light of morning seeped into the room to compete with the yellow radiance from the oil lamp, Dorothea lifted her head and gazed at the man beside her. She'd long since gone from sitting on the edge of the bed to lying curled up beside O'Hare, her hand still in his. Someone—probably Ron—had tucked a blanket around her.

Now Ron dozed in a chair across the room. Dorothea could not claim she'd slept, just flitted in and out of awareness, pricked by constant stabs of fear.

For a long time she'd heard voices coming from the men downstairs and wondered why they stayed, until she realized they must be on guard in case someone came to finish the job and make sure O'Hare did not survive.

Had he survived?

She stared at him in alarm by the sickly combination of real and artificial light. If anything, he looked worse than last night, the bruises deepened in intensity, the swollen patches more extreme. She leaned close, striving to catch his shallow exhalations, for he breathed so low she'd several times during the night been sure he'd slipped away. *He lives.*

Did this first light count for morning? Did the doctor's promise hold true, and would Hare now survive?

At least he felt warm. She squeezed his fingers and touched his throat, one of the few places he wasn't bruised. When she did, she felt the beat of his heart, steady as the blows her father struck in the forge.

Thinking of her father brought tears to her eyes. For a moment she longed so for him, with his kindness and quiet strength, she could barely see straight.

What would he want her to do now? Keep strong, be patient. Fight for the man she loved, tooth and nail if she had to.

The certainty of that allowed her to blink the tears from her eyes. She whispered, "You're not going anywhere without me, understand?"

O'Hare's lips moved as if in response. He couldn't open his eyes, both of which had swollen shut, but Dorothea felt convinced he heard her.

"Hold on to me," she told him. "This is the worst of it. You're strong, so strong. And I promise you're not alone."

Ron stirred in his chair, got up and moved to the side of the bed. "He's alive?"

"Yes."

"Well, girl—you kept him anchored to you all night. That's a good sign. What now?"

Dorothea tried to think beyond the victory of this moment, to peer into a day she could barely imagine.

"I'm sorry, Mr. Murray, but he'll have to stay here. It's too soon to move him yet. I think he should see the doctor again. I'd be much happier if he woke up."

"And once he does?"

"See what he remembers, so we can file charges. Either way, I think we need to get the police here today. Justice must be available to all in this city—Irish or otherwise. But I'll accept vigilante justice as well as the official kind."

Ron smiled crookedly. "He's responding to your voice—see that? His fingers twitched, and his eyebrow, too. Maybe he likes that you're still fighting."

"So long as he keeps fighting also." Dorothea thought furiously. "Can you send someone for the coppers as soon as it's full light? And if I write a note, can you get my things from my rooming house? Sorry to do this to you, but I may have to stay here too, for the duration."

Ron shrugged. "I don't mind, girl. And I'm not planning to open up today. I think one of the lads is still sleeping downstairs."

"Good. Because this is the hero of Irish Boston. And it's time for the Irish of this city to stand up and be counted—with the police or without them."

****

By noon, Dorothea had spoken to two strapping police officers who came to Ron's shop and listened impassively to her account of things. Even though one of them had red hair and a thick Irish brogue, they displayed little sympathy and made no promises.

"Happens every day, miss," said the second, non-Irish officer. "We rarely have any success chasing down the perpetrators. Say—aren't you the reporter who wrote all those stories about O'Hare—D. R. Sinclair? There's a story about you in a special edition today."

So there now. As soon as the police departed, Dorothea asked Ron to send for a copy of the *Guardian*. They read the headline together, in stunned surprise:

Dead Hero of Irish Boston
Was In Romantic Relationship With Reporter.

Color mounted in Dorothea's cheeks as she read the account, written by one Jeremy Winton—of course—describing how a female employee on the *Guardian* staff had deceived them into believing her a legitimate reporter, all while pursuing her own agenda.

The young woman in question had been meeting the subject clandestinely at the den of a fortuneteller in this city and clearly slanted her stories to present her lover in the most favorable light. The Guardian *apologizes to its readers for perpetrating a false image of the subject, who has disappeared and is believed dead.*

Dorothea looked up from the page and met Ron Murray's stare. "They think he's dead!"

"Not for long," Ron grunted. "There's too many know he's here."

She swore softly, using words of which her mother would heartily disapprove. "Those blackguards—they used me and my features to sell all those papers, and now they fall back to their usual stance, that of hate-mongering. What's more, this edition must have gone to print last night. How could they have known about the attack, unless…"

"Unless one of the lads talked, which they wouldn't."

"Or Dr. Liffey."

"Don't think he would, for all his sins."

"If he were drunk…"

"Even if he were drunk."

Dorothea tapped the byline on the paper. "Maybe the *Guardian* orchestrated the attack on Hare. What if

Winton not only knew about the contract but initiated it?"

"Would he?"

"Mr. Murray, I believe Montgomery and Jeremy Winton would do *any* vile thing to further the profile of this paper."

"What are you going to do about it?"

"Have my things been brought from the boarding house yet?"

"Yes. The old harridan there went off on the lad— said to tell you never to darken her door again."

"She needn't worry."

"But your reputation, miss—if it gets out you're staying in an all-male household…"

"Oh, it will. Everything will out. And my reputation be damned. What worries me is protecting O'Hare once Boston at large figures out that he's not dead—and just where he is."

Ron's eyes narrowed. "You have something in mind, haven't you?"

"I intend to write a story." She turned her eyes on Hare, who lay so quietly. She hated to leave him even for a moment but didn't know how else she could carry on the fight. "Then I'll have to go out for a while."

"Not on your own, you won't. It's not safe. I'll come with you."

"No, Mr. Murray, you need to stay here, organize a guard, and look after him."

Ron snapped his fingers. "I think I have just the solution. You write your story, girl. Leave the rest to me."

****

"Are you sure he's not dead?"

The woman who stood at Hare O'Hare's bedside smelled of the finest French perfume and shone with sartorial splendor from her tiny, silk-clad feet to the smart hat perched on her golden head.

Dorothea, who had dressed hastily in clothing dragged from Mrs. Bennett's and couldn't find a hat at all, eyed her with mingled emotions. Marielle Dickenson, so Ron Murray declared, was a good friend of Hare O'Hare's. And, obviously, a woman of some means.

"The story's all over town that he's been murdered and thrown in the Charles River," the vision went on miserably. "And I must admit, he looks dead enough."

She might appear a great lady, but Irish rolled from her tongue and shone from her eyes when she gazed at Dorothea—an indefinable something visible despite the tears.

"It was a close thing last night. The doctor seemed to think the head injuries would carry him off."

"So—you're she? The woman in his life? And you're also the one who wrote those marvelous stories. It's all anyone's talking about, and nearly a riot out there. Won't be long till he's located. What then?"

"I believe all this was orchestrated by management at the *Guardian*."

Marielle's eyebrows flew up. "So what's to be done?"

"I mean to expose them. I'll go there this afternoon and resign, and then I'll take my story to the *Herald*." Dorothea indicated the sheets of paper on the table beside the bed. "But I need someone to accompany me—someone of unimpeachable credentials."

"Me?" Marielle's eyebrows soared higher still.

"Mr. Dickenson will have a fit."

"If you're not willing…"

"I didn't say that. I'd love to take on those hate-mongers at the *Guardian*, with their lies. I have to say, I was that surprised at them running a series of stories putting someone like Hare in a good light. But they were just selling papers."

"I believe they were behind the attack."

"If you've a way to bring the bastards down, count me in."

"Mrs. Dickenson, if you don't mind me asking—what's Hare O'Hare to you?"

Marielle smiled tenderly. "You mean, Timmy? That's the name he went by when we first met, you know. We were in service together. Ah, don't look so surprised; I was naught but an Irish lass laying the fires and scrubbing the pots of those better than me. Only they weren't better." She glanced at the man in Ron's bed. "He may well be. And you. But in any case, I love him like a brother, if that satisfies you."

"I have three brothers. They're maddening, but I'd give my life for them."

"Or your reputation? You've no idea what it's like out there, Miss Sinclair. The city's gone mad. But if you—or he—need me, I'll stand by your side."

"Then, Mrs. Dickenson, better gird yourself up for a battle."

Chapter Twenty-Three

"He's alive?" Montgomery Winton's eyes nearly started from his head with the words. He gave Marielle Dickenson a doubtful look before turning his gaze back on Dorothea. "And you're in collusion with him. So my son was right."

Before Dorothea could reply, Jeremy Winton sneered, "It won't take much to find him—we need only trace your movements."

"Go ahead," Dorothea responded. "You'll not get near him."

She had left a crowd of men—all Irish and vowing on their lives to guard Hare O'Hare—at Ron Murray's. She and Marielle had fought their way, in Mr. Dickenson's fine carriage, through a city thronged with people. Outside the offices of the *Guardian*, the throng had become a mob, some folks throwing stones, many hollering at each other. The two women had pushed their way through to find both Wintons together, and Dorothea had promptly served her notice.

Now she looked Jeremy Winton in the eye. "I know you took out the contract on Hare O'Hare's life. How do you think that will look in print?"

His sneer intensified. "You have no proof."

"Are you sure? This city has a lot of ears, many of them Irish."

"Don't be a fool. There were no witnesses."

Montgomery Winton cleared his throat. "Not that my son admits any guilt." He switched his gaze to Marielle Dickenson. "Why are you here, madam? And does your husband know you're colluding with ruffians?"

Marielle lifted her head proudly. "My husband—an influential man, as you know—supports my efforts toward equality. And I'm here to tell you if anything else happens to Hare O'Hare—or Miss Sinclair here, for that matter—I will be the first to place blame."

"A thousand men in this city want O'Hare dead. Now that it's known the reporter who showcased him is nothing more than a trollop who raised her skirts for him—"

Marielle stiffened. "His fiancée, you mean."

"Eh?"

"Get your story straight, gentlemen. I have it on the best authority they're to wed."

Both men looked at Dorothea who nodded woodenly, though color flared in her face.

"Before that happens"—Marielle leaned forward confidingly—"we mean to bring you down."

They were outside again and making their way to the Dickensons' carriage before Dorothea asked, "Why did you say that?"

Marielle eyed her closely as they climbed into the carriage and shut the door against the rowdy mob. "It's the truth, isn't it? You love him, and you have the look of a woman who means to get what she wants. I can't imagine you settling for anything less than marriage."

"Yes," Dorothea breathed, "if—if he's going to be all right."

"Hare O'Hare?" The elegant Mrs. Dickenson

snorted. "He's too hardheaded to die now."

"And what about your husband? The vile Winton is right—he'll be furious you've involved yourself in all this."

Marielle gave a smug smile. "Lass, I've recently told my husband, Mr. Dickenson, I'm going to bear him his first child. He—and I—are convinced it's a son. Nothing can make him angry with me. Where to now?"

"The offices of the *Herald*, where I mean to make them an offer—if they'll see me."

"Ah, clever lass. You just go in there telling them all you're Hare O'Hare's fiancée and the woman who wrote all those stories. They'll see you, right enough."

Mrs. Dickenson's prediction ultimately proved true, though it took some time to get through the hierarchy at the exalted *Herald*. Dorothea and Marielle at length returned to Ron Murray's, tired but victorious, to find a crowd there also, and a scene of chaos.

Most of the businesses on Ron's block had closed; a mob of thugs faced off against the Irish guarding the place, and several of Ron's windows had already been broken. The rioters scattered when Mrs. Dickenson's coachman—who also happened to be Irish—laid about him with his whip, and the two women made it safely inside.

"By all the saints, Dorothea, you can't stay here— nor keep Hare here," Marielle declared.

Dorothea had no chance to reply. Ron seized her hands.

"Thank God you're back, miss. He started to go down right after you left. I think we're losing him."

Dorothea never later remembered climbing the stairs. She entered the room to find O'Hare shuddering on the bed, his head cocked at an unnatural angle.

"Oh, God. What is it?" She climbed onto the bed and clasped both his hands.

"He's seizing," said Marielle, who'd followed her up. "He should be in hospital."

"No hospital will take him now," Ron replied.

Marielle shed her bag and gloves. "Then send for the bloody doctor. I don't care what it costs."

Ron ran out, and Marielle approached the bed. She laid a steadying hand on Dorothea's back.

"Probably not safe to move him anyway."

"Not yet. Do you think he's dying?"

Marielle caught her breath audibly. "Don't know. There now, he's quieting. It's your touch he's wanting, lass. Clearly, you can't leave him again."

Disregarding the tears streaming down her face, Dorothea vowed, "I won't. I swear to God, I won't. But as soon as he can be moved…" Her throat closed.

Marielle looked at her curiously. "Then what?"

"I'm taking him out of this damned city. I'm taking him home."

****

Five days passed before Dr. Liffey and the second doctor whom Marielle summoned—a specialist called Morgan—reluctantly agreed Hare could be moved. By then, south Boston lay in a state of virtual riot.

Dorothea's exposé piece had run in the *Herald*, followed by several others researched by the *Herald*'s own staff. Jeremy Winton had been named as a participant in the beating deaths of several Irishmen and was under investigation for contracting the attack on Hare.

"The lads he hired will squeal eventually,"

Marielle predicted, "if only to protect themselves. They'll not take the fall on their own, you mind."

Marielle had done her best to get Hare admitted to a hospital, but none would accept him, citing the likelihood of riots ensuing outside their doors. So he'd remained at Ron's under twenty-four-hour guard, mostly provided by workers from the docks and the waterfront, and usually with Dorothea at his side.

All the while, he'd failed to regain consciousness, though neither did he repeat the terrifying afternoon when he seized. He lay as one peacefully sleeping unless Dorothea left him, when he became agitated and his condition swiftly worsened.

"He knows you're here, lass," Marielle told her. "He wants you by his side." She swept Dorothea with her bright, blue gaze. "Lucky lass, to have won such a heart."

Had she attained that prize? Dorothea couldn't be certain, though she slept beside him in the bed and ate her meals there too, all between helping Marielle force water between Hare's lips and, several times, a shot of whiskey, the price of which his admirers and guards had taken up in a collection.

"If that don't keep him alive," Terry Gallagher declared, "he's not Irish. Water o' life, that is."

He lived, though his bruises continued to darken and look worse rather than better. Dorothea spoke to him in a steady stream of words until even she, noted for her ability to chatter, grew hoarse. She whispered to him during the endless nights, lying with her fingers against his chest so she could feel his heart beating. Once or twice she wept.

Meanwhile, the *Guardian* ran stories defaming her

character and calling her "O'Hare's lightskirt," even citing the fact that the couple had been seen embracing on a street corner. The *Herald*—who had initially agreed to run more stories under Dorothea's byline—sent word that under the circumstances they had reconsidered the offer, at least for the foreseeable future.

Even Molly sent word telling her to lie low and to look well after her recovering patient, at whom threats were still being leveled. So on a bright May morning, with Dr. Liffey's approval, she packed up her scanty belongings, hugged both Ron and Marielle goodbye, and loaded her charge into Marielle's carriage, bound for the train station and Maine.

Marielle had paid their fares and also hired two guards to accompany them. They were on the platform, jostled on all sides and alert to any danger, when Dorothea felt a touch on her arm.

Sybil, having apparently materialized from nowhere, stood gazing at her with fathomless dark eyes. "A warning," she intoned.

Both guards mobilized; Dorothea held up her hand. "It's all right, I know her. Sybil?" Her stomach dropped. "You've seen something?" Tell me. Will he recover?"

"There are many wounds, some visible and some invisible. His body will mend. His spirit embarks on a harder journey."

"Harder? Than this?"

"Guard him well. Hold him in your love. He will fight against you. You fight still more fiercely, understand?"

Dorothea nodded warily. She felt weary, spent, but

she knew how to fight.

To her surprise, Sybil embraced her in a fog of patchouli. "Angel, you are an angel—his angel," she said.

****

"Almost there," Dorothea whispered to the man beside her. It seemed she'd said the words a dozen times. They'd taken the train to Augusta and on northward, staying overnight in Bar Harbor before embarking on the packet boat for her hometown, the small port of Lobster Cove.

Now she sat close beside the pushchair Marielle had purchased for the journey and peered out the windows of the boat, hungry for a first glimpse of home. Hare sat in the chair, his head tipped to one side, face still a mess of healing cuts and bruises.

She hoped her father would be waiting for her at the harbor. She'd asked Marielle to send a message ahead, saying only that she was returning home with an injured friend and citing the boat on which they expected to arrive.

She longed for the sight of her father, with his big, strong frame, his silver-streaked black hair, and his kind eyes. She expected full well to fall apart when she reached the refuge of his arms.

A miracle she'd kept her emotions under control this long…

"Almost home," she told Hare yet again, and squeezed his fingers. He turned them over and clutched at her hand, the best response she'd had from him yet.

The packet boat slowed and made the wide turn into the harbor. Dorothea got to her feet and strained to see through the moisture-speckled window.

Her heart accelerated.

"God! Oh, God, Hare—they've all come. Not my mother, no, but there's Pa. And Dougie and—oh, Jo! And their children as well, all three of them."

Tears blinded her then, and she had to stuff her fist in her mouth to keep from sobbing. Love resided here with arms open...

She looked at the man beside her. "They're going to love you too." How could they do anything else?

Chapter Twenty-Four

The two body guards maneuvered Hare's pushchair onto the wharf before they turned back for the packet boat. They would return to Bar Harbor when the boat did, and thence to Boston, which now seemed so very far away.

Dorothea looked at her father approaching along the wharf, hitched up her skirts, and ran. Laughing and crying, she threw herself into his arms.

"Pa! Oh, Pa."

"Dora, wee angel." Scotland still rode her father's voice in a deep burr even after so many years in Maine. Dora wouldn't have it any other way. She loved his rumble and the scent of him, like singed metal, leather, and home. The whole wharf smelled like home, as a matter of fact—salt fish and seaweed mingled with wood smoke.

And her father's arms, wrapped around her, felt like heaven. She had to force herself to pull away far enough to look into his eyes.

"I've brought someone."

He searched her face, his deep blue gaze questioning and concerned. "So your message said. I don't doubt there's a story in it."

She laughed unsteadily. "With me, there always is. Jo!" She turned from her father to embrace her friend, who clutched her so tight it hurt wonderfully.

"How I've missed you." Jo, too, wept happy tears, her beautiful, dark eyes awash and brilliant. "What you been up to? Making waves in Boston?"

"You have no idea. Douglas!" She embraced Jo's husband in turn before waving wildly at the pushchair and the man covered to his chin. "I'm so glad you're here. If you and Pa could just help me get my friend, Hare, out to the house—we've had ever so terrible a time."

"'Course I will," Douglas answered with one of his rare smiles. "We came prepared, even brought a wagon."

"Then let me introduce you." She seized her father's hand and drew him to the pushchair. "Not that he'll be able to acknowledge you. He was severely beaten, as you can see, and hasn't spoken or even reacted to much. But I know he hears what you say. Why, only moments ago he squeezed my hand…"

"Breathe, Dora," Jo urged. "It will be all right, lamb."

"I know. I know it will."

Or perhaps not. For upon catching sight of Hare O'Hare on the wharf, her father froze like a man hit between the eyes by a hammer, staring.

"Sweet heaven!" he exclaimed. "What did you say his name is?"

"Why, what's wrong?"

"His name, lass."

"Hare O'Hare. Only that's not his real name. Pa?" For her father had gone white and looked more upset than she'd ever seen him, even that time Archie broke his leg so badly. "You look like you've seen a ghost."

"That's because I have. Holy Jesus." Her father

turned to Douglas. "Here, lad—do you know who that is?"

Douglas narrowed his dark eyes and shook his head. Then he shot Pa a close look and drew a breath. "You don't mean—? It can't be…"

"What?" Dorothea nearly jumped up and down with frustration.

"Aye. I know his name," Pa said. "That's Timothy O'Shea. He was born here in Lobster Cove."

****

From that moment, when Dorothea's father spoke the words "Timothy O'Shea," her life became all madness and argument. And to think she'd spent days longing to return to the bosom of her family, hoping she might find a measure of peace.

None here, it seemed. They began arguing there on the wharf and didn't quit.

"Not Timothy O'Shea." Douglas took it on, he who so rarely disagreed with Pa. "If he's who I think you mean, it was never 'O'Shea.' That's Timothy Grier."

Grier? But that was Douglas's last name.

Dorothea's eyes narrowed. She knew the name O'Shea, of course, though tied with the appellation "Declan." People in Lobster Cove still talked about Declan O'Shea—a now-deceased sailor and lobster fisherman far too charming for his or anyone else's good. Declan O'Shea had been her mother's first husband, back before she'd ever imagined marrying Pa, and there'd been some terrible scandal. But how could Hare—her Hare—be part of all that?

"Listen to me." She waved her arms wildly. "We can't let him sit here on the dock. Pa, what makes you think he's…"

Her father's eyes rolled like those of a spooked horse. "I've only to look at him. Even with all the bruises he's—he's the spit."

"But—"

"Lass, how can I take him home to your mother? The very sight of him will shatter her."

"His name's not O'Shea, though." Douglas stepped forward and peered at Hare. "His name would be Grier, Timothy Grier, and he's my half-brother."

Jo stared at her husband. "You saying that man there's your brother? The one you told me about?"

"Half-brother," Douglas repeated carefully. He glanced at his own children, who stared. "We had different fathers."

"This the one you told me your ma took away with her when he was little? Well, then." Jo's eyes widened. "If he's your brother, I reckon he's coming home with us."

"Oh, Jo." Dorothea felt limp with relief. "Thank you."

"Never mind, honey. You just bring him along, understand?"

Jo went ahead with the children, and Douglas brought the cart around. While he maneuvered it, Dorothea said to her father, "I can't believe this is true. But even if it is, I can't imagine Ma would shut her door to him. She's the kindest, most generous woman I know."

"Better he goes to Dougie's," was all her father replied.

"What happened to him?" Douglas asked, once he and Dorothea's father had Hare loaded in the cart.

"There was an assassination attempt—he was

beaten senseless because he stood up for his rights and those of others. He's a hero in much of Boston."

"You don't say."

"I appreciate you opening your door to us, but this doesn't really help the situation much," Dorothea told Douglas on the ride to his place. "Not if Ma means to avoid him." The house Douglas had built for his family lay less than a half mile up the coast road from the Sinclair family home. It lay, in fact, part way to the old O'Shea cottage, now long abandoned. "And I don't understand my father reacting this way."

"Don't you?" Douglas returned.

"No."

"Dora, sometimes when things come out of the past, they look even bigger and more awful than they really are. You know how it was for Josie when her past caught up with her."

"That was different."

"Was it? I'm not so sure. Some terrible things happened back before your parents got married. I don't know all of it, except that Declan O'Shea was involved."

At the Griers' house, Douglas and his son Daniel— the Griers' oldest child—helped Dorothea get Hare inside, while Josie changed the sheets in Daniel's room, which she said the boy would not mind vacating.

"He'll enjoy camping out," Jo assured Dorothea when she protested. "That boy will use any excuse to sleep outside. Sometimes I swear he's all Penobscot."

She took a good look at Dorothea, set down the sheet, and held out her arms. "Come here, girl."

"Oh, Jo!" Dorothea wept. "All the way here I could only think about how I much wanted to be home and how desperately we need a safe place for Hare to heal. He has to get stronger, to come back to himself. Otherwise I don't think I'll be able to go on."

Josie mopped Dorothea's cheeks with the hem of her apron. "You love him?"

"You can't imagine how much. But everything's such a muddle. If Ma..."

"You listen to me. You love him, and your ma will just have to come round. Because you, I, and she all know very well—there's just nothing more powerful than love."

Chapter Twenty-Five

"Where is he?" Lisbeth Sinclair blew through Josie's front door like the tail end of a hurricane, shoulders set and eyes resolute. "I want to see him."

Behind her back, her husband shot Douglas an apologetic look. He carried his youngest child, Andrew, in his arms. The other two boys, Archie and Alasdair, who were fifteen and sixteen respectively, were away with their boat on a fishing jaunt. Much as she wanted to see them, Dorothea could only think that for the best. There were already enough opinions clogging the air.

Josie stationed herself in front of Lisbeth, her diminutive form a frail but staunch barrier. "He's upstairs, and yes, you can see him. But the man's in a bad way, Lisbeth. If he is who Rab thinks—and I can't help believing this is all some crazy misunderstanding —it's none of his fault anyway."

"I know that." Lisbeth waved her hand wildly at Dorothea. "But he's my daughter's lover, Josie. Her *lover*."

Dorothea gasped. "Who told you that?"

Her father dug a crumpled paper from his pocket and thrust it at her. She unfolded it and read: *Emergency. Coming home with injured lover.*

"Marielle sent this," she tried to explain. "I never… That is, I told her to let you know I was bringing an injured friend."

Her mother stared at her. "Then you're not in love with him?"

Dorothea flushed. Her lips worked over a denial that wouldn't come.

"Oh, God, it's just like the past come over again." Lisbeth seized Rab's arm. "Dorothea, have you slept with him?"

"Mother, get hold of yourself. It's not what you think. He may not even be who you think."

"Well, let me see." Lisbeth caught up her skirts and made for the stairs, with Josie right behind her and Dorothea bringing up the rear. Lisbeth marched across the landing to Daniel's room, only to stop in the doorway as if someone had struck her. She gripped the door jamb, and her fingers turned white.

Douglas and Daniel had put Hare in Daniel's bed, where his copper curls made a bright splash of color against the white pillowcase. Eyes closed and perfectly motionless, he once more looked dead.

Lisbeth gazed upon him, gasped painfully, and folded to the floor in a faint.

****

"Tell me all of it," Dorothea bade her mother. "You'll have to, now."

Lisbeth, ensconced on the daybed in the Griers' parlor, where her husband had placed her after carrying her back downstairs, said nothing. She merely stared at Dorothea out of a face nearly as pale as Hare's.

They sat alone, everyone else chased from the room by Josie.

Concern and consternation still had Dorothea's pulse elevated. She'd never known her mother—a strong and quite practical woman—to faint under any circumstances. This did not bode well.

With false calm, she went on, "I already know parts of the story. You were married to Declan O'Shea before you married Pa."

"I was so young. Young as you are now. I thought I knew what I wanted, and he had that charm, that Irish charm…"

"There was some kind of scandal." A miracle, really, that no one had spoken of it in all this time.

"He cheated on me. We'd only been married a year, but he fathered a child on the barmaid at the Hogshead—Maggie Grier—and another on a woman who lived in that big house out on the bluff. He was as false and fickle as the sea, and it nearly cost me everything."

Dorothea reached out and grasped her mother's hand. "Maggie Grier was Douglas's mother, right? And the child Declan O'Shea fathered on her—you think that's Hare?"

Lisbeth shuddered involuntarily. "I first saw him when he was a few months old—the spit of Declan with that red hair and the same tawny eyes. Timmy, she called him."

Dorothea's heart sank. "Listen, Ma, that man upstairs might be your first husband's illegitimate son. That doesn't mean he's anything like him—faithless and fickle. You don't know what Hare, that is, Timothy, is like. He never even met his father."

"Why do you call him 'Hare'?"

"That's the name he's taken, working in Boston—his persona, if you will."

"A lie."

"No. He's a man of honor, a hero fighting for the

rights of his fellow workers and for the welfare of families in the city. And I"—Dorothea drew a shaking breath—"can think of no finer future than to stand beside him."

Lisbeth blinked. "Honor? The son of Declan O'Shea?"

"Ma, if he is Declan O'Shea's son—and it does seem as how he must be—he's inherited nothing from him but that red hair and the unusual eyes."

"Impossible."

Dorothea's temper, on tap always at any show of injustice, flared. "Shall I tell you about the impossible? He and I spent the night together. Oh, don't look at me that way—I'm a grown woman, and I love him. I would have given myself to him then—given all of myself. He wouldn't have it; he was too set on protecting me, afraid I'd made a hasty decision."

Lisbeth's lips worked, but no words came.

Tears flooded Dorothea's eyes. "And now he's so sore hurt, attacked for what he believes, and I can't get him to come awake. I was sure that, once we got here, the peace and safety of this place would heal him. But he just lies there, Ma, and I can't reach him. I can't!"

Lisbeth sat up and gathered Dorothea into her arms.

"There, now," she whispered, just as she had when Dorothea was little and had skinned her knee. "There, now."

"Jo says nothing is stronger than love." Dorothea wept. "But even my love can't call him back."

"Hush. Jo's right. I know that's true."

"Ma, his heart's so hungry for love—starved. I've never known one hungrier, except maybe Dougie's. I kept telling myself if I could just feed his heart, answer that hunger with enough love, he'd wake up. But now I don't know."

Doing a complete turnaround, Lisbeth raised Dorothea's chin and met her eyes. "Don't you fall apart on him now, Dora. If love's what he needs—well, then, keep giving it to him. He never had any from his father, and precious little from his mother, as I recall."

"Then, Ma, you promise not to hate him?"

"How can I, dear? He's already in your heart."

****

Hare and Dorothea walked together along a shore in a far distant place—a rough, grassy track that led northward toward the past. Or was it the future? He found he couldn't tell, only that peace existed here, and Dorothea's voice floated constantly in his ears.

To be sure, the lass loved to talk.

On their right lay rocks verging the wide, gray-blue ocean—the exact color of his Dora's dreamy eyes— stretching away to a barely perceived horizon. Or maybe that wasn't the ocean at all. Perhaps those were Dora's eyes and he now existed only inside her, for he had lost any real connection to the world.

Yet she held him—or her voice did; it kept him from slipping away, as did the comfort of her presence. Her hands stroked his hands or his face, now covered in beard, and her love flowed into him wherever her fingertips met his skin. Her love wrapped around him like the blankets she tugged up to his chin and the warmth of her body when she lay beside him.

As soon as she left him—and that wasn't often—he began to slip away. His moorings creaked, and he felt himself slide backward from this path they trod together into oblivion. Then his heart called to hers.

"Here," she said now. "Just another sip." He felt the rim of a cup against his lips. "It's broth. Mind you don't choke. Doc Stevens says if you don't eat you'll just grow weaker, and we can't have that, can we? Drink it for me."

He did, obligingly. He would do anything she asked of him.

"Where are we going?" He indicated the path ahead.

"Into the future. No, don't you dare look back, Timothy Grier."

"You know my name."

"I know everything about you."

"What's up ahead?"

"Who can tell? I know what's not there, and that's the past. When we reach that place up ahead, you'll see it's ruins, all ruins."

"Will you be there with me?"

"I'll always be with you. Now, drink."

"Again?"

"Again."

"Hold me."

She did—so close in the night he couldn't tell where his flesh ended and hers began. They walked together through the warm night, with stars spread above like the painted ceiling at Sybil's.

"How long has it been?"

"Days and days." She sounded like a child when she said that. Yet no child, this. Deep in the night he kissed her, or thought he did.

"Here, my love—let your brother lift you up so we can change the bed."

187

Brother?

Strong arms bore him upward, and a voice rumbled. Dora answered, and he struggled to open his eyes.

"I want to see him. And God, lass, I want to see your face."

"Then come awake. All you need to do is wake. I'm here."

"What will happen when we reach the future, Dora mine?"

"We'll get married."

"Will we?"

"Oh, yes. Don't you remember I asked you, before?"

"What did I say?"

"Your lips said no—they're foolish lips. But your heart said yes, and I'm only listening to your heart. I already have my dress planned. So you better not disappoint me, Timothy O'Hare Grier. Open those eyes and make me the promise."

"I wish I could."

"I will talk you into submission. Tell me how soon you want to marry me."

"Soon. Today."

"We can't till you open your eyes. And how many children do you want?"

"Children!"

"Oh, Mr. Timothy O'Hare Grier, there will be children. I'll make sure of it."

"Ah, then—three. Five. Ten."

She laughed, but he could hear the tears.

They reached the end of the path. To the right lay a clutter of rocks fronting the sea, beyond a stretch of shingle beach where the water washed in like an eager lover reaching.

To the left…

"What's that?"

"The ruins. This is the place. The place where the past and the future meet."

It had once been a cottage, most likely. Now only the chimney stood, stone on stone, like a stark finger piercing the sky. The roof had fallen in and the walls crumbled.

His past had crumbled.

He couldn't feel the pain of it anymore. All he could feel was Dora's hand in his and her love filling him, filling his heart to overflowing.

She turned toward him on the path, tugged at both his hands so he faced her, and gazed into his eyes. What beautiful eyes his Dora had, brimming with strength and determination. They put the ocean to shame.

"It's time," she told him.

"For what?"

"For you to choose. You can see the past is gone—there's no going back, and it can't reach you anymore. But I'm here, and I'll never desert you. Choose. Choose me and open your eyes."

She kissed him then, the kiss he'd awaited for days. The warmth of her poured into him, heat enough to melt away the last of his doubt.

With joy filling him, he opened his eyes.

Chapter Twenty-Six

"Just like sleeping beauty," Dora said, satisfaction filling her voice.

Hare looked down at himself ruefully—weak as a child and marooned in a bed, all busted up. He still couldn't completely fathom what had befallen him.

"Not much of a beauty, am I?"

A grunt came from the direction of the door, where his brother stood. *His brother. Douglas.* Just one of the things to which he'd had to become accustomed since Dora dragged him from unconsciousness two days ago, claiming him with her kiss.

Douglas Grier couldn't look more different from him if he tried. Tall, and with muscles built in the blacksmith's forge, he had dark, wavy hair, dusky skin, and steady, dark eyes. Not a man to say much, Douglas—unlike Dora—but his gaze met Hare's now in a speaking look.

"You're a pitiful specimen, Tim," he pronounced. "Better get up on your feet soon."

"I mean to. I will." A smile tugged at Hare's lips. "You want me out of your house?"

Douglas shook his head. "Don't mind about that. You two stay as long as you like."

You two. Hare inhaled deeply, ignoring the protest from his half-knitted ribs. It seemed he and Dora now made a pair, and no one meant to argue it. Certainly not

Douglas or his beautiful little wife with the wide, compassionate eyes, or any of their three children.

Two pretty girls and a boy almost as tall as his father. He was an uncle—well, half-uncle.

And he lay in his brother's house, in this pleasant room with the yellow walls and the blue curtains embroidered all over with bears because Daniel—his nephew—had a liking for them. The boy's mother, Josie, had done that for Daniel out of love.

Only imagine a ma who'd do such a thing… Yes, he lay in the very lap of love.

Dora, who sat beside him on the bed with his hand in hers, said, "Doc Stevens is coming back this afternoon. After that, you're getting up. Do you hear me?"

"I hear," he told her tenderly. He would always hear; her voice and touch had anchored him, her kiss had drawn him home.

He wished she'd kiss him again.

Douglas cleared his throat. "When you two get to looking at each other that way, I figure it's time for me to leave. But Tim, I did want to ask you…"

Hare looked at Douglas. His brother had decided to call him *Tim*. He had so many names, all twisted together just like his past.

"You say my ma's dead?"

"Yes. She had some kind of sickness in her belly. Do you remember Gene Browne? He was with her till the end."

Emotions passed through Douglas's dark eyes, a whole line of them. "They stayed together? Who'd have thought? She was…happy, then? She had a happy life?"

Hare grimaced and pushed himself up on the

pillows. "I wouldn't say that. They argued like two cats in a sack, and if there ever was any love"—he glanced involuntarily at Dora—"it wore out long since. But they did stay together. You didn't miss much, for what it's worth."

"At least they raised you."

Pain lurked in those five, simple words. Funny how easily Hare could now sense others' emotions. This man still had a boy inside him—one who'd been abandoned.

"If you can call it that," he said seriously. "A lot of drinking on their part, hunger and neglect on mine. I got out as soon as I could support myself."

Douglas nodded. "Thanks." He looked at Dora. "I'll leave you now to—" He waved an expressive hand. "But, Dorothea, don't forget your ma and pa are waiting to come up."

She smiled ruefully. "How could I forget?"

Douglas grinned suddenly, which made his face change amazingly, and went out.

Hare turned to Dora, who gnawed at her lip. "You're thinking about what your ma's going to say when we tell her we're getting married." He still had trouble keeping it all straight in his mind—that this little town on the coast of Maine where his Dora had grown up was the same as where he'd been born. That the man his ma had declared to be his father on her deathbed—one Declan O'Shea—had at one time been married to Dora's mother. A right prince of a man, by all accounts, and certainly no father of whom to be proud.

How would Mrs. Lisbeth Sinclair feel toward him? How would she feel about her cherished daughter wedding the byblow of the man who'd cheated on her with the town barmaid?

It made for a prickly situation, and no mistake. It wasn't as if he and Dora were related by blood, she being the daughter of Lisbeth's second husband, but the implications went deep.

He gazed into Dora's eyes and said, "Any chance you could stall this discussion with your parents till the doc says I can get up? I'd much rather face them on my feet like a man."

"I'll see what I can do." Like the answer to his prayer, she leaned forward and kissed him. For several breathless minutes the world fell away. Happiness rose in a bubble to his head.

"Well," he whispered as he cradled her face between his hands, "at least one part of me's up."

****

Lisbeth Sinclair would not look Hare in the eyes. It wasn't as if she hadn't tried—he believed she'd done her best when he entered the parlor on the arm of his brother. She just couldn't, so she kept her gaze locked on her folded hands, which rested in her lap.

Rab Sinclair's eyes, though, were all over him, probing and measuring. The kind of man Hare liked on sight, Rab all too obviously remembered his father.

And he hadn't liked him.

Douglas settled Hare in a chair and mumbled, "I'll leave you to it," before beating a hasty retreat. Dora pulled up a second chair near enough so she could hold Hare's hand, facing her parents—presenting a united front.

Rab Sinclair spoke gently. "So the doc's given you his approval to be up and around. Must have been one hell of a beating you took."

"I don't remember much about the attack—nor any of what came after. Dora's said she thinks I must have been on my way to a bar called Dooley's. But yes, they did a job on me." He felt his jaw gingerly. "At least, judging by the injuries."

"They left you for dead." Dorothea sounded angry. "There was a price put on him."

"So you've said." Rab and his wife exchanged glances. Hare could guess what Lisbeth must think of her precious daughter keeping company with the kind of man who suffered assassination attempts.

"There's a lot of unrest in Boston over this question of equal pay for the Irish," he told Lisbeth steadily. "But I have a good job; I'll be able to support Dorothea pretty comfortably. Of course, she'll want to work—or write. I'm not about to discourage that. Can't put a bushel basket over that kind of light."

Lisbeth paled. Her eyes came up to meet Hare's at last. "You don't actually have an accent. I can't get used to that—no charming Irish accent rolling out of you."

"Ma, he's not *him*." Dora leaned forward. "He's not his father."

"But he looks so much like him. Especially his eyes."

"Ma'am, I'm not my father," Hare reiterated. "I never even met the man."

Lisbeth nodded, and her eyes filled with tears. "I'm sorry. Of course you're right. This is hard for me, so hard."

Rab reached out and clasped her hand, but his gaze held Hare's. "So you're saying you mean to marry our daughter?"

"If she'll have me."

"I'll have him," Dora said almost in the same breath.

"And," Lisbeth took it up, "you want our approval?"

"I would like it, ma'am, but I intend to marry her with or without. I know I'm not worthy. You don't have to tell me that. But after all the hard things that have happened in my life, luck's finally smiled on me, because she's chosen me—cursed if I know why. I love her. For me it's gone way beyond love. I need her. I don't suppose you'd understand…"

Lisbeth got to her feet and went to the window. "I understand."

"So I'll give her till I'm on my feet, really on my feet, to change her mind—"

Again Dorothea interrupted, "I'll not change my mind. Ma, I know you don't like this. I can only imagine how it must feel to you. He's not the man you might pick for me. But you made your choice—"

Lisbeth turned abruptly. "A disastrous one, the first time—based on nothing more than charm and patter and good looks." She waved a hand at Hare wildly. "But little substance."

Dorothea surged to her feet also; the two women faced each other, alike in many ways, similar height and build, one fair and one dark. Dorothea trembled with her intensity. "I nearly lost him. I had a taste of what it would be like with him gone from my life. I have a second chance, just like you got, and I'm taking it—with your approval or otherwise. I can't help who he is. Neither can he. He's going to be my husband and the father of my children, so—"

"Children!" Lisbeth gasped. She looked like someone had struck her hard, and her gaze flew to Hare's once again.

Rab rose and seized her arm. Somehow, Hare pressed to his feet also. The last thing he wanted—the very last—was to cause a breach between his Dora and her parents.

He cleared his throat. Everyone stared at him, including Josie Grier who, he'd been aware for some minutes, hovered in the parlor doorway.

"Ma'am," he said humbly, "I would never do anything to hurt your daughter, would never betray her or let her down in any way. She's honored me with her affection and helped me in ways I can never tell—since I don't have her gift with words—and answered a hunger so deep I never knew it existed. Not till I laid eyes on her, anyway. But if being with me is going to cost her anything—the approval of her family or your affection, well…"

He hesitated, not sure he could speak the words, but his heart forced him to go on. "I'm willing to give her up." His lips twisted in a rueful smile. "I imagine she'll have something to say about it, though."

Lisbeth Sinclair stared at him, her eyes wide. Before she could speak, Josie Grier came bustling in, straight up to Lisbeth's side.

"Hear that now," she said. "Would his father have made such a selfless offer? Not from all you've told me about him. Lisbeth Sinclair—you're the kindest woman I know. You were able to accept me, a Negress, when Dougie brought me to you, for the sake of love. Surely you can accept him for the same reason."

Lisbeth looked at Hare again. Something in her gaze softened. "The past is gone, after all. And this is Dorothea's story to write. Anyway, I know my daughter. She's already set her heart on you." She drew a deep breath. "So I suppose the only thing I can say is —welcome to the family."

Chapter Twenty-Seven

"I have something for you."

Josie Grier peeked into the room where Dorothea Sinclair prepared for her wedding. The yellow room, filled with sunlight, matched Dorothea's mood. All the windows stood open, admitting the warm sea breeze of a beautiful June afternoon.

A June bride—quite traditional, and not what Dorothea had ever imagined for herself. But Hare had agreed they should marry here, where they'd both been born, on the condition he could be well and truly on his feet first.

They'd stayed at the Griers' home even though Lisbeth had offered them Dorothea's old room. They'd stayed partly because Dorothea could see a relationship developing between Hare and his brother and partly because she still wasn't sure how her mother would cope with having Hare underfoot morning, noon, and night.

Daniel, delighted with the situation, had gone a bit native, moving to the woods and relishing his independence.

The townsfolk—many of whom remembered Declan O'Shea all too well—had been slightly less accommodating. From their reaction to Hare, he had to be the image of his father. No wonder Lisbeth looked like she'd seen a ghost every time she encountered him.

But Dorothea knew how hard Lisbeth tried, for her sake.

She turned now from the mirror and smiled at Josie. One advantage of staying here had been time spent in the company of her best friend.

"A gift?" she echoed.

"A wedding gift, sort of." Josie slipped in through the door and extended her hands, in which lay…

"My hat!" Dorothea stared. "It's the one that got ruined in Boston. How did you—?"

"It's not the same hat. I recreated it, close as I could remember. I know how much that hat meant to you, seeing as how it brought you and Tim together."

"Oh, Josie. It's beautiful, and the perfect touch for my outfit." Dorothea set the hat on top of her black hair, which Josie's clever hands had swept up into a fancy series of waves.

Josie's eyes widened. "I didn't mean for you to wear it today. What about your veil?"

"I don't think I'm a 'veil' sort of bride. That's one of the reasons I love Hare, Jo. He understands I'm not like other women, and it's all right with him."

Josie laughed softly, tears in her eyes. "And he's able to endure those moments when your tongue comes unhinged and you talk and talk at him?"

Dorothea grinned. "Better than that, I think he actually likes it."

"Then you better hang on to him, child, and don't let go."

"I mean to—just like you held on to Dougie. Well, how do I look?"

"Breathtaking. And you know that hat goes with the dress." Dorothea's mother had put everything else aside to stitch her daughter a simple gown of lace and satin—not white but palest blue, as suited Dorothea's inner yen to be different.

"What do you think he'll say when he sees me?"

"That man better be careful or he'll fall right back down. Better hope his best man has a good grip on him." Josie's expression grew tender. "I can't tell you what it's meant to Dougie, being asked to serve as best man. And having the two of you here. I think it's healed something inside him, getting to know his brother after all this time."

"And Hare, too. They both needed that. And they've hit it off, haven't they?"

"We'll need to stay in touch after you go back to Boston. You sure you have to go back?"

Dorothea nodded solemnly. "We have work to do there. But I hope we can come home soon." Dorothea blushed. "Maybe for the birth of our first child. Speaking of which, wise Mrs. Grier—do you have any advice for me?"

Josie laughed. "Just have fun. Oh, yes, and love him—love him so hard you can't stand it and sharing yourself seems natural as breathing. Nothing to fear, then."

"Can I tell you a secret, Jo?"

"Sure, honey."

"I can't wait."

****

"Well, Mrs. Timothy Grier, I hope you're not thinking of making all this into a story."

"Hmm?" Dorothea replied to the smile she heard in her new husband's voice rather than his words. She loved it when he spoke to her that way, with the affection spilling from him as if he couldn't contain it all.

They lay in the bed in the yellow room with their fingers linked, just as their bodies had so recently been—not one but two times. Heaven had touched down in Dorothea's soul, and she felt nearly too happy to speak.

He went on, musing, "I saw that look in your eye earlier today."

"What look is that?"

"Like you were keeping track of everything and tucking it away till you could get to a pen and paper. How your brothers looked—like they were going to a hanging rather than a wedding. How the townspeople stared and whispered—how proud your father looked."

"Proud and handsome."

"And handsome. And your ma—no wonder you're so pretty, Dorothea Grier."

"What about Dougie? The only time I ever saw him cry before was the night Daniel was born. Today he just stood there beside you, all straight and tall with the tears rolling down his face."

Hare shifted in the bed and turned to face her. His hand stole to her breast.

"You're not going to mind leaving them all?"

"Of course I'll mind."

"Then…"

"My place is with you. And your place is in Boston. Like I told Jo, we've work to do. We need to get back and cook up a way to curtail the activities of those Wintons. Heck, I wouldn't mind bringing down the whole *Guardian*."

"You're right. We can't have that weasel Jeremy

back on the streets."

"He gives weasels a bad name. Besides, Ron's probably missing you. Too bad he couldn't leave the shop to be here. And Marielle—no doubt she's showing by now. I hope—" She stopped speaking abruptly.

"What, angel?"

"I hope I'm showing soon. I can't wait, I simply can't wait to carry your child. Of course, that won't keep me from working. I figure I can do feature articles for magazines till the folks at the *Herald* come to their senses, outlining the injustices that still need addressing in Boston. And—what do you think of this—I mean to start a new novel. It's what I always truly wanted to do, you know—like Louisa May Alcott. Only in this book my heroine will be a woman of Boston, someone like Deirdre Gallagher. I'll show her trials and strengths, and the unfairness of—"

"Hush."

"What did you say to me?"

"Hush, Mrs. Grier."

"Well! I just got done this afternoon telling Jo how much you like it when I natter on."

"So I do. I like everything about you, including that sweet little freckle on your left breast." He caressed the place in question with his thumb, and all Dorothea's senses leaped to attention. "I just thought you might want to put in some work making sure of that baby you've requested. You see, Dora mine, I took a vow this day to give you everything I can. Everything— you—want." He punctuated the last three words with kisses. "And I do believe I can provide that."

"Well, but"—she seized him with both hands— "are you sure you're fit for all this activity?" She caressed his cheekbone and his ribs. "Just think of your poor bones…"

He began to laugh softly. "Did I not seem fit a few minutes ago?"

"Yes."

He directed her hand downward. "Don't I seem fit now?"

"Oh, yes."

"Then, Mrs. Grier, you remember this: I love you beyond all reason, and I'm about to prove it. But don't you dare write it down."

A word about the author…

Born and raised in Western New York, Laura Strickland has pursued lifelong interests in lore, legend, magic and music, all reflected in her writing.

She has made pilgrimages to both Newfoundland and Scotland in the company of her daughter, but is usually happiest at home not far from Lake Ontario, with her husband and her "fur" child, a rescue dog.

Author of Scottish romances *Devil Black*, *His Wicked Highland Ways*, *Honor Bound: A Highland Adventure*, and *The Hiring Fair* as well as The Guardians of Sherwood Trilogy consisting of *Daughter of Sherwood*, *Champion of Sherwood*, and *Lord of Sherwood*, she has also published three Steampunk romances, *Dead Handsome: a Buffalo Steampunk Adventure*, *Off Kilter: a Buffalo Steampunk Adventure*, and *Sheer Madness: a Buffalo Steampunk Adventure*, two Christmas novellas, *The Tenth Suitor* and *Mrs. Claus and the Viking Ship*, and a Valentine's novella: *Ask Me*. Her Lobster Cove Historical Romances include *The White Gull* and the novella, *Forged By Love*.